2ND STRIKE

SCHOCK SISTERS MYSTERY SERIES, BOOK 2

MISTY EVANS
ADRIENNE GIORDANO

2nd Strike, A Schock Sisters Mystery, Book 2

Copyright © 2019 Misty Evans & Adrienne Giordano

ISBN: 978-1-942504-35-1

Publisher: ALG Publishing, LLC

Cover Art by Fanderclai Design

Formatting by Beach Path Publishing, LLC

Editing by Gina Bernal, Elizabeth Neal, Patricia Essex

Please Note

1

Charlie

*A*fter a crazy, surreal day at work, the last thing I want to do is jump into a fresh case.

The universe has different plans.

Welcome to my world. I'm Charlize Schock, private investigator, and, like my last name, shock is what I experience as the next few seconds unfold.

The air outside is that in-between state of early spring—not truly warm, yet not cold either. The night is cool and crisp, but I feel the heat of summer approaching.

My sister, Meg, and I are just leaving the office when a young boy wheels into the parking lot of Schock Investigations on a bicycle.

"Who's that?" she asks.

She survived an attack by a psychotic killer earlier today and needs a relaxing bath and twelve hours of uninterrupted sleep. I could use the same.

"No idea." I motion for her to stay at the car and grumble when she ignores me. We walk forward as I ask, "Can I help you? Are you lost?"

"Are you Charlie Schock?"

Under the parking lot's solar lights, he looks to be a teenager. Curfew's in an hour. The whole thing seems off, my gut warning me he saw the news about us and Billy Ray Wilson and wants an interview for his class project. "We're closed. Call our number and leave a message. We'll get back to you." *Or we won't, if you're a freak.*

Some days, I hate myself for being so paranoid, but it comes with the territory. As a former FBI profiler with a Ph.D. in forensic psychology, the list of nutjobs in my background is extensive. My meter is sensitive and it's in the red zone at the moment.

"I left a message. Several in fact." He gets off the bike, releasing the kickstand, and reaches into his jacket. "You didn't return them."

Gun. It's my first instinct and I back up, putting my hand on the butt of my own weapon. At the same time, I throw my other arm out to protect Meg. Instinct. She's my little sister.

The kid pulls out a folded piece of paper and holds it out to me. "I need your help."

The magic words. The ones I can never resist, especially when I move closer and see the pleading look in his eyes. Maybe the shadows under them are from the ghostly lighting, or maybe he hasn't slept in a while either.

My fingers itch to reach for the paper hovering in the air between us. Meg moves by my side, sizing up the situation.

"With what, kid?" I ask, dropping my protective arm.

"I need you to explain this." He unfolds the white, official looking sheet and holds it out again. "I've been over these tests results a dozen times, and I understand what they mean, but they don't make sense."

I see DNA markers, three sets of them. "Why is that?"

He shifts his weight, those eyes still imploring me to take the paper. "I'm Ethan Havers. Do you remember me?"

It only takes a heartbeat for the name to click and then I look the boy over from head to toe. "Carl and Lily Havers' son?"

He nods.

The first kidnapping case I caught as an FBI agent.

"Wait, Carl Havers, the talk show host?" Meg studies Ethan inquisitively. "I did the age progression on you."

Fifteen years ago, Carl was an up and coming reporter for a local D.C. news channel. His good looks and winning on-air personality moved him swiftly into the anchor seat, where he's been ever since. His wife, Lily, also a TV personality, gained wide audience appeal when she became pregnant with their first and only child.

"I chose to do my final project in Biology on DNA," Ethan says. "My *family's* DNA. But there's a big, big problem, Charlie."

I take the results from Ethan's hand. A few days after he was born, he was kidnapped by his babysitter. I returned him to his parents seven years later after tracking her down. Meg did, indeed, create the image of what Ethan looked like at that time, and it led to me finding him. "What is it, Ethan?"

But I know before he even answers. The DNA markers of Carl, Lily, and Ethan dance before my eyes. Meg studies them over my shoulder.

"They don't match," the kid says softly. His voice is rough, almost as if he's about to cry. "My DNA didn't come from my mom and...from *them*."

"Holy shit," Meg says.

Holy shit is right.

I look up and meet his eyes, speechless. My stomach bottoms out.

"You returned me to the wrong parents, Charlie," he whispers. "I'm not Ethan Havers."

Meg looks at me as if she can read my mind. She can. "I'm sure there's an explanation," she says.

I'm sure there is but it could be a damn poor one. I bite back my frustration that the Havers refused to do DNA testing eight years ago when I brought Ethan to them. They were convinced he was their son and all the evidence pointed to that as well.

"Why don't you go on home?" I suggest to Meg. My thoughts are running ahead of me, ninety miles an hour. "Ethan and I have some catching up to do."

"The hell I will." She motions at the back door to our building. "We need to get to the bottom of this."

Meg is my sister, my best friend, my rock. She's an accomplished forensic sculptor who barely survived Billy Ray's attack a few hours ago, but here she is, ready to dive into my mess as if it's just another day—or night at this point—at the office.

If the results in my hand are accurate, there is no bottom to find. There will be hell to pay, and my ass will be the one doing it. The Bureau won't take any responsibility, nor help me fix this, since I no longer work for them.

"My dad did a news segment where he submitted his DNA to see what countries his family originated from and revealed the results on his show," Ethan says softly. "He convinced Mom to do it, too. It was really interesting because Dad thought he was English—British, you know?—and German. His results showed he's forty percent Norwegian and doesn't have a drop of German in him."

Many people discover similar results. I've seen it hundreds of times as a genealogy hobbyist. "That's why you wanted to do it for your final."

He nods. "Most of the kids already knew my parents' results because of the news segments. It was fun." His gaze goes to the paper. "I thought it'd be cool to see how much of each of their DNAs I had."

I take a deep breath, stopping the spinning hamster wheel

in my brain. I'm getting ahead of myself. *I did not make a mistake eight years ago.* I saw the age progression Meg did and it was nearly an exact match to Ethan. There's a simple explanation. There has to be.

Sleep would allude me now even if I went home and crawled into bed. Meg and I exchange a glance and she nods, reading my mind again. Looks like we have a new case.

Except we don't take cases from minors.

Hmm.

Giving Ethan a reassuring smile, I motion for him to follow. "Let's go inside."

Schock Investigations contains three offices, Meg's art/workroom, a tiny kitchenette, bathroom, and the receptionist area. I tap buttons on my phone to turn off our security and use my key to let us in.

Meg goes in first, slapping on the lights, Ethan in her wake. His backpack is high-end, expensive, just like his designer jeans and sneakers.

Although Meg and I are both single with no kids, she's got a maternal streak and chats with him about the weather, curfew, etc., as I lock us in, turn the alarm back on—the brush with a serial killer has my paranoia in overdrive—and grab a water for Ethan.

Meg sits in one of the two chairs across from my desk. Ethan takes the other. His backpack now rests against the desk, and he accepts the bottle when I hand it to him, but doesn't open it.

I'm far from being a DNA expert, but my side hustle is reuniting lost families, which involves studying genetic results and family trees. While my father is the one who ignited this hobby for me when I was a kid, Ethan's case all those years ago is the reason I plunged back into tracking people's ancestry as an adult.

Everyone is quiet as I study the paper. It's not a complete

evaluation, but it paints a clear picture all the same. There is a brief, impersonal written analysis and I read it several times, trying to wrap my brain around this situation.

When I finally look up, Meg stares a hole through me. Ethan has set the water on the desk, crossed one ankle over his knee and is picking at the rubber on his sneaker.

"I can't tell my parents about this," he says quietly. "They're having problems...with their marriage...and this would be, like, too much on top of everything else." He glances at me, guilt clouding his face. "It's my fault—I mean, I'm the reason it's on the rocks. Seeing this?" He points to the paper and shakes his head. "Way, way too much."

Too much, indeed. Unfortunately, his parents will have to be told if we're going to pursue the truth.

Ethan uncrosses his legs and sits forward, rubbing his hands on his jeans. "How did you figure out who the kidnapper —Amelia—was?" he asks. "How did you know for sure I was theirs when you found me?"

He deserves to know, but his parents should be the ones to share that information. The case is long closed, and many of the specific details where suppressed from the public, even though it was big news in the media. He's probably already done a search and found numerous pages of hits. It garnered world-wide attention, but legally, I'm on shaky ground, unless I get the FBI, and/or the U.S. district attorney to sign off on it.

"Look, Ethan, inaccuracies crop up from time to time. The legitimate testing companies do their best to provide accurate information, but samples get contaminated, software glitches occur, or there can be a biological element that doesn't jive, and just needs further analysis."

"Like what?" There's a glimmer of hope in his eyes.

"Have you studied chimeras in biology class?"

He shakes his head.

I give him a Charlie Schock assignment. "Go home and look

up genetic chimeras. There's a famous trial case—Lydia Fairchild. Tests proved her children weren't biological matches even though she claimed they were. Eventually, prosecutors discovered she carried two sets of DNA—weird, right? But it's possible, and that type of thing can screw up results. I'll look into the lab and verify their procedures, but the thing I recommend is running a new test at a different facility and comparing the results. That'll require consent from your parents and samples from all of you again."

He reaches for the backpack and withdraws a paper and a plastic zipper bag with three hairbrushes in it. "I have the original consent form and hair from all of us."

Smart kid. "Sorry, but no. I need new consents, but let's not do anything until I talk to the lab and look into possible reasons the results don't match, okay? Go home, stop worrying—there's a simple answer to this—and I'll call you tomorrow."

"But—"

His protest is cut off by a sharp dinging from my phone. The security camera out back has caught someone pulling into the parking lot. I open the app and watch as JJ Carrington parks and gets out of his big, black SUV. He saunters to the back door, waving at the camera.

I shut off the alarm and sigh.

Meg sits forward, her face creasing with concern. "What is it?"

It was only two days ago when Billy Ray walked into our offices as if he owned the place. I'm not the only one whose paranoia is going crazy right now.

"Nothing," I lie. JJ is the U.S. attorney for D.C., and some days I swear he can read my mind as easily as Meg. Have I somehow conjured him up by thinking about this case?

At my sister's distressed look, I ease her mind. "It's JJ."

The man is my Achilles' heel. My body gives a little cheer

seeing him, and I curse under my breath. "I'll be back in a moment."

At the door, I unlock it but only open it far enough to speak to him. "What?"

Over six feet with dark hair and eyes the color of a perfect summer sky, he gives me a sexy grin. "Can I come in?"

"Meg and I were just on our way out."

"I swung by your place and you weren't there. Just wanted to make sure everything is okay."

Right. I can read his mind too. He wanted to see if I'd let him stay the night. "Everything's fine." Another lie, but I'm not ready to tell him about Ethan. "I'll call you tomorrow."

Without another word, he grabs my hand, and pulls me out the door and into his arms. "I can't wait until then."

2

Meg

While my sister is busy doing whatever it is the two of them do, I study Ethan's face. His chestnut hair falls below his ears and curls at his neck. His eyebrows are dark, an exact match to his hair, and his deep brown eyes hold the misery of a teenager lost in too many thoughts.

I give him a gentle smack on the shoulder. "Ethan, we'll figure this out. Between Charlie and me, we know enough DNA experts to form a summit."

For a few seconds, he plucks at the leg of his jeans, his gaze fixed on his moving fingers like locked-on radar. He won't look at me and I suspect he's holding back tears. Proud young man. Probably also terrified. He has a right to whatever roller coaster of emotions he's feeling right now. His world has been flipped, his identity along with it.

Before I speak, I take a second to consider the situation.

This, even for the Schock sisters, is a new one. Add in the exhaustion that comes from surviving a psycho killer's attack and I'm hardly at my best.

Ethan's father is a nationally known newscaster turned morning show host. At seven each morning, Americans welcome Carl Havers into their lives. A respected journalist who's visited war-torn countries, interviewed presidents, kings, and bombing victims, Carl stopped chasing big stories after Charlie and the FBI brought Ethan home almost eight years ago. In an effort to rebuild his family, he walked away from the adrenaline rush— and awards—that came with ground-breaking stories opting instead for a seat at the anchor desk. Now he's home each night. For his son, who he'd missed years with.

For that, people love him.

His looks don't hurt. A classic heartthrob, his borderline Greek God features send housewives everywhere into fantasyland each morning.

The network execs sure don't mind. Not with their top ratings.

To the outside world, Carl and family have sifted through devastation to create a perfect life.

And now his son sits in front of me, wondering who the hell he is.

"Ethan?"

Finally, he peers at me, his gaze shimmering and my heart snaps in two. "I don't know what to do," he says.

"Of course you don't. That's okay. Right now, I want you to take a breath. We're here to help you."

"I can't tell my parents. I can't. My mom is..."

This is tricky territory. Ethan is a minor and he's asking us to withhold information from his parents. Given the situation and his father's high-profile status, I'm fairly astounded that I am, in fact, willing to be his co-conspirator.

My logic is simple. If the press gets hold of this it will be, in short, a feeding frenzy. Reporters will gnaw the flesh off this kid's bones and we can't let that happen.

I lean forward. For a hundredth of a second, I pause. Reconsider what I'm about to say. I'm no rocket scientist, but I am smart.

It appears, so is Ethan.

He could run with any information I give him and that responsibility will land on me. Worse, my sister will eviscerate me. The lecture alone will wreck me.

Is it worth the risk?

I stare into his shiny eyes and hate the misery. The boy needs answers and we can help him. "Okay, bud, here's an idea. A couple months ago we worked with a genetic genealogist."

He blinks at me. "A what? I mean. I know what they are, but what's the genetic part?"

"She's basically a genealogist that's leveled-up. She understands DNA and uses databases to find potential matches. Once she sorts those out, she starts narrowing down relatives. We solved a cold-case based on her building a family tree from a DNA analysis."

Ethan perks up, his dark eyes widening a fraction. I have his attention. I knew I would, but the stab of guilt doesn't stop me.

"Cool," he says.

"Yep. On the last case she worked for us, she found our suspect through a woman who'd entered her DNA test results into a free online database. The genealogy companies charge, but the public one doesn't."

A publicly accessible database, GenCo, is the brainchild of a couple of amateur genealogists who wanted to provide folks with a free resource to track their heritage. As word of the site grew, more and more people uploaded their DNA results into the GenCo database. What started as a hobby for a couple of retired guys, turned into a controversial tool for law enforcement.

Now, anyone loading results could potentially link a distant relative, like the cold case we'd worked, to a crime.

Somewhere in the process, privacy laws became a gray area that might be exactly what we need to protect Ethan's identity.

"So," Ethan says, "*anyone* can enter their results?"

They sure can. "Pretty much. Users have to be eighteen though."

"Crap." He shakes his head and winces. "Sorry. My mom hates when I use bad language."

I wave that off. Heaven knows I've heard and said a whole lot worse. "Don't worry about it."

"What happened with that case? The one the genealogy lady worked on?"

"We got insanely lucky. Ann Marie entered our suspect's profile into the public database and found a strong paternal match. We looked into all the men in the woman's lineage and eventually found a cousin whose DNA matched what was found on the victim."

At that, Ethan straightens up. "We could put my results in."

"Not without your parents' permission. You're not eighteen."

The kid slumps back. We're stuck here. As much as I'd love to have Ann Marie enter his results into GenCo, I can't. Morally, it's not right. Not without his parents. They all deserve the truth, but at what cost?

"Ethan, I know you don't want to tell them about this, but I think you have to. It's their life, too. And they can help you work through this. If you were my son, I'd want to know."

He whips his head back and forth. "No. I won't. I *can't.* Mom will freak. She's crazy right now. I don't know what she'd do and if something happens it'll be my fault and—"

"—whoa." I put my hands up to silence our visitor. The

energy in the room explodes and my already frayed nerves crackle. Ethan's anxiety, if left unchecked, will escalate. Having suffered from panic attacks, I know the insanity that comes with them. The hell of raging, irrational thoughts that leave the sufferer gasping for air and terrified. "Take a breath, Ethan. In through your nose and out your mouth. Nice and easy."

I keep my voice low and even and soon he's breathing in sync with the cadence of my words. After a minute, he lifts his chin and pushes his shoulders back.

"Are you okay?"

He nods. "Sorry."

"Don't apologize. This is a horrible situation for someone your age. An adult would struggle with this. Believe me."

"What do I do now?"

I check my watch. Almost ten. We have to get him home. "It's late. I think you should go before your parents start to worry. In fact, let's throw your bike in my van and I'll drive you."

"No. They can't see me getting out of your car."

He whips his head back and forth again. I'm losing him. I reach over, squeeze his arm. "Relax. I'll drop you off down the street. They won't even see me."

He pauses, obviously considering my suggestion. There's no way I'm letting him trek home on his bike in the dark. Not in this condition. He's distracted and worried and if something happened to him, I'd never forgive myself.

"Okay," he finally says.

A chime sounds. After a recent break-in, my sister upgraded our security system and now all the entrance doors make a different sound. The chime is our back door.

Seconds later, Charlie appears in the doorway. "Hi. Sorry."

"No problem. Is the Emperor gone?"

JJ's nickname in the world of D.C. law enforcement is the Emperor of Cold Cases. I'm not sure there's been one yet he hasn't thrown every ounce of his energy into. There's something in him that won't let a victim go without justice. He isn't always successful, but it doesn't keep him from trying.

Charlie snorts at my use of his nickname. "He just left."

"You're sure? I told Ethan we'd put his bike in my van and I'd take him home. If JJ is out there, you need to get rid of him before he sees us with a kid and starts asking questions."

My sister gives me the bitch-face she's perfected over the years. "Meg, I watched him drive off. Believe me, he's the last person I want getting wind of this. We don't need the U.S. attorney involved until we know more."

"Perfect." I hold up the reports Ethan just handed me. "I'm about to copy these and then we'll go."

"Okay. If we can get Ethan's parents to agree to another test, I'll reach out to a couple private labs and see if they can put a rush on those hairbrushes. With any luck, we'll have an answer in a few days and can compare the new results with the old ones." She turns to Ethan. "And then we should know."

3

Charlie

"Assuming the DNA test results are legit and the lab didn't make a mistake, I may need a lawyer," I tell Meg after we drop off Ethan and meet back at our duplex.

We face each other from across our respective front porches, the matching outside lights illuminating our faces.

Hers is tight with fatigue and concern. She's a few inches shorter than me, about the same weight, but she has curves. Me, not so much.

Concern for me and Ethan shows on her features. Before she can say anything, I continue. "First, we have to decide if we're taking him on as a client. Legally, we can't call him that. Minors can't hire investigators without their parents' consent. They can't enter into legal contracts, and since he's my problem, it may be better if I handle this situation alone. I can shield you from the fallout as much as possible."

Her fatigued face is sharp with sudden anger. "Charlize Lauren Schock, what the hell is the matter with you?"

This confuses me. "Huh?"

She rolls her eyes as if I'm dense. Maybe I am. "We're helping the kid—*we*, as in you and me." She waggles a hand between us. "We're a team, that's how we work. Stop with the nonsense about shielding me. I helped with Ethan's case all those years ago; I'm as much involved with it as you are, and minor or not, he's our client. He's not a stranger who walked in off the street. In my book, this is simply a continuation of the original case. We'll involve them if and when the time comes, but until then, Ethan is our first concern."

I love my sister and her viewpoint on so many things, but I score extremely high in the responsibility department. Part of me wants to run over and throw my arms around her for the support; the other wants to protect her at all costs.

"If this is screwed up, and he isn't their son, I could be in big trouble, Meg. I'm not taking you down with me."

As in, I'll ruin my outstanding reputation, look like a failure in front of the world, lose JJ, and potentially send Schock Sisters Investigations down in flames.

Somehow, I know she's reading my mind. She feels the low grade panic I'm fighting.

Her face softens. "Why didn't the Havers do a DNA test when you found Ethan?"

"Everyone urged them to, but we had the kidnapper's confession and your age progression sketch was a close match."

On the seven-year anniversary, Carl had been involved with a nationwide missing kids' organization. He went to the FBI and asked if he could get an age progression drawing to take on the show, hoping to bring media attention once more to his quest. Meg was well-known for her skills and my boss sent Carl to her. Her sketch got us the tip about where Ethan was living.

She nods. "The next door neighbor recognized him from my work, right?"

"When we confronted Amelia Norris, she admitted kidnapping him. She'd been his babysitter. Claimed his mother didn't want him, but after her confession, she committed suicide."

Meg snaps her fingers. "That's right! She shot herself in front of Ethan, didn't she?" A shake of her head and a sigh. "The boy needed therapy and had a hard time adjusting to his new life with Carl and Lily. No surprise."

I ache for him, even now. "The media attention was overwhelming and Lily insisted he was hers. The evidence backed it up." I shrug. "We couldn't force them to perform DNA tests."

"How could this be your fault, then? If anyone is to blame, it's Carl and Lily."

I lean on the railing, grabbing the rope my sister has thrown me. "The thing is, these are famous people with a story the world loved eight years ago and still does. The FBI will look for a scapegoat and so will Carl and Lily. Since I'm no longer with the Bureau, they'll throw me under the bus, sure as I'm standing here. It was my first case as lead investigator, and I know I did everything by the book, as did the rest of the team, but if he isn't their child, we now have two mysteries to solve— who is the real Ethan Havers, and who are the parents of the boy who came to our office tonight? Without the kidnapper, we don't have answers to either."

"Then that's where we start," she says. "Until we determine for sure Ethan is not who we believe him to be, we start with the crime that occurred—the kidnapping—and focus on learning more about Amelia Norris. No one can stop us from doing that, and she's the key to both mysteries."

The FBI didn't worry too much about her—the kidnapping was solved, the boy returned. Happy ending, closed case. Move on to the next hundreds of open kidnapping cases.

I still remember how I walked on air for weeks after that. I'll never forget the joy on Lily's face when I accompanied the social worker to deliver Ethan to their house. He was scared and very shy, but when she knelt down and opened her arms to him, he fell into them like he'd known her his whole life.

How could he *not* be her son?

"Do you still have the notes from that case?" Meg asks.

"You know I do." I have file cabinets of my personal notes on all the FBI cases I worked. They're organized alphabetically and by year, cross-matched and color-coded, in my spare bedroom. "I'll get them out and take them to the office in the morning."

"Good. Get some sleep." Meg unlocks her front door. "If we end up needing a lawyer, we'll get that DelRay woman. She's an ass-kicker."

"Jackie?" We worked a case with the defense attorney a few months ago, and that title is putting it mildly. Again, I could hug my sister. "You're brilliant. I'll give her a call first thing tomorrow, see if I can put her on retainer, just in case."

Meg yawns but pauses before she goes inside. "What did JJ want?"

What does he always want? I almost say it out loud. Instead, I skirt the idea he wanted to come home with me to celebrate the fact I'm still alive and he looks like the star he is in the judicial world because Meg and I caught a serial killer with his help.

I also don't mention the soul-sucking kiss he laid on me in the parking lot. "I scared him pretty bad today taking on Billy Ray. He wanted to double check I was okay. That's all."

The mention of the killer makes Meg shiver. "I hope the bastard rots in prison. I'm glad JJ came by to check on you."

She winks and goes in, calling, "Goodnight."

"Goodnight," I mumble and let myself into my side of the duplex. I reset the alarm, lean back against the door, and close my eyes.

My home is dark and quiet, the first peace I've had in a

while. I should take a hot bath and go to bed, get some sleep like Meg instructed. The next few days will most likely be chaos.

That's my plan, until I walk past the spare bedroom. I flip on the overhead light and the filing cabinets—lined up like diligent soldiers—gleam like magnets. I feel their pull.

Twenty minutes later, I have the Havers' files spread on the floor. I grab a glass of wine and start reading.

4

Meg

By nine, I'm on the George Washington Memorial Parkway with sunshine streaming through my windshield as the remains of rush hour traffic winds down. I've already been to the office and helped myself to a few pieces of information from Charlie's file on Ethan.

Now, I'm off to Alexandria for a visit to Jerome. Otherwise known as my weed dealer.

He's actually not one, per se. He buys medicinal grade pot from someone he trusts and shares with me. That's what friends do, right?

Jerome texted at seven—he's a morning person—to let me know *the goods* were available.

This arrangement works well for us since I'd like to avoid getting busted buying pot. I'm chicken that way. I'm in a partnership with a beloved sister, which means I have a responsibility to her. That includes not bringing embarrassment to a business that deals with law enforcement—and a U.S. attorney —on the daily.

As I pull into the right lane, a car roars by and I tap my brake. I've been in D.C. long enough to know Mr. Mercedes is about to cut in front of me to get to the exit first. Which is exactly what happens. People. Always in a rush.

Afterward, I come to a stoplight. The Mercedes is right in front of me and I shake my head. If Jerome were here, we'd make snide comments about how far the idiot got by cutting me off.

It's one of the things I love about Jerome. We share a sarcastic humor. It doesn't hurt that we're both creatives interested in forensic art.

And, hello? We also turn to the occasional pot brownie or joint to settle us down. Where my issues are anxiety based, Jerome has ADD. His attention span is zero and for someone in our field, that's an issue. Weed relaxes him. Helps him focus.

I pull into the small parking lot of his single-story apartment complex and park near his unit.

His front door swings open and I get a sick thrill, that fleeting buzz in my core, from the fact he was waiting for me. He stands there in torn track pants and a long-sleeved T-shirt. His honey-blond hair is slicked back—wet from a shower probably since he doesn't blow dry—and his cheeks show at least two days of stubble.

My mind skitters back to the first time I saw him at a workshop on the anatomical method.

Something happened.

That something being attraction. Not like JJ/Charlie, let-me-rip-your-clothes-off attraction, but a quiet pull that made me insanely aware I am A.) female and B.) like an orgasm or five every now and again.

Worse, he was funny and smart and I enjoyed him way beyond the sexual aspect. My rotten luck, because all that respect for his brain threw the idea of multiple orgasms out the window.

I haven't had a ton of relationships, but I know sex screws things up.

Big time.

And I'm not sure I'm willing to lose his friendship if any intimacy between us bottoms out. I actually care too much to risk it.

Twisted as *that* is.

Plus, I don't have time to devote to a man. And Jerome deserves devotion.

So he's my friend instead of my lover. My go-to guy when I need someone to talk to.

Or do a sketch when I can't be objective.

I keep my gaze on his until I reach the lone step to his doorway. "Good morning."

As I approach, his hazel eyes lock on mine, a touch of mischief lighting them. I often feel naughty when our "drug deal" goes down and he likes to tease me about it.

"Good morning," he says. "You look tired."

He slides the door wider and I breeze past. "I am. Couldn't sleep and I was out of brownies."

"I saw the news," he says. "You should've called me. What with the serial killer and all."

Sufficiently chastised, I nod. "It was late."

He closes the door and ushers me to the small living room where his sparse furnishings provide enough seating for company. His own art, and a sketch I did of the Silver Tail river, adorns his walls. Beyond that is a galley kitchen. Across from it, the lone bedroom door is open and I spot his unmade bed.

I avert my gaze. I can't think about that and Jerome in the same thought. I may self-combust.

I plop onto his sofa, dropping my messenger bag next to me. "How busy are you today?"

To supplement his artist's income, Jerome works part-time at a small gallery in D.C. The money isn't great, but the hours are flexible and allow him to explore his creative endeavors. Including the occasional composite sketch for various law enforcement organizations. Or, in this case, me.

He settles into a hand-me-down wicker chair my sister wouldn't be caught dead in and wipes fuzz from the top of the coffee table he made out of repurposed wood. Then he peers at me, his smile flashing. "I'm free. Want to entertain me?"

I sure do. Except, a sudden bout of pissiness assails me. Blame it on the fatigue from the last couple weeks because I suddenly feel like nothing in my life is as it should be.

I'm unmarried. No prospects in sight. Don't even get me started on my chances of being a parent.

I lean in, returning the smile. "Are we ready to go there? Truly?"

Waving me off, he sighs. "You're no fun."

This is news to him? After all the talks we've shared about my anxiety? My obsession with the sculptures of dead people that adorn my office?

My pulse kicks up and I inhale before I say something stupid. But...screw it. It's time for me to control my life, not the other way around.

"I know. But I care about you. I might even say I love you. And if we're going there, we're *going* there."

Dang, I really needed that pot brownie last night. If I'd had it, I wouldn't have all this emotional garbage churning me up.

His jaw drops. "You..."

Might as well dive in. "Don't freak. It's not..." What? I shake my head. *I don't even know what it is.* "It's not let's-get-hitched love. It's more-than-a-friend love though."

His shoulders slump, but I'm not sure why. Is it relief? Horror?

Disappointment.

After three years of friendship, I may not know him as well as I think.

Good one, Meg.

This would be why we've been circling each other. This unknown place. This awkwardness.

"I didn't mean—"

He holds his hand up. "It's...okay. I actually think I understand."

"Good. Then you can explain it to me."

The smile appears again and my pulse settles. This is why he means so much to me. He knows what I need, when I need it.

"We're stuck, Meg."

Oh, thank God. All this time we've never discussed it. We've sat in this apartment, occasionally getting stoned and laughing ourselves silly but never once have we slipped about our feelings.

We're either both idiots or two people who have amazing respect for a relationship we cherish. "We *are*. Part of me wants to do something about it."

"And the other doesn't. I know. So, what? We keep doing this?"

How the hell should I know? I shrug. "I guess. At least until we're sure it's what we want."

"How long will that take?"

"You're asking me?"

A laugh rumbles free and the whiteness of his teeth nearly lights the room. I like that. That I make him happy.

"Okay," he says. "At least we know where we stand." He raps his knuckles on the table. "Back to my schedule. I work tonight. What do you need?"

Perfect answer. I pop my bag open and slide Ethan's file out. "I think you'll like this. Can you help me with a composite sketch?"

After thumbing through the file, I pass him a photo of the Havers' infant son. I refrain from handing him the FBI's age-progressed image of what that baby would've looked like as a fifteen-year-old. I don't want it to taint his interpretation.

"The baby was kidnapped fifteen years ago. Charlie worked the case when she was a fed. I'd like you to do another progression showing what he'd look like now."

His bottom lip rolls out. "Why don't you do it?"

I give Jerome the summation of Ethan's visit, leaving out specifics of who he is. All I give him is Ethan's first name and then I lay the line on him about client confidentiality.

"Holy shit," he says.

"Precisely. This boy needs to find out who his biological parents are. We told him we'd help. Charlie wants an age-progression done to see if," I point to the baby's photo, "that child looks like him. And since I've seen Ethan, I can't be objective."

He sets the two documents down and sits back, propping one ankle over his knee. "I'm not as good as you."

I've heard this from him before and each time I hate it more than the last. Our talent is...different. Not better or worse.

He's more fluid with color and shading where I'm better with finer details. The curve of lips, the flair of noses. Jawlines.

Together, Jerome and I are the perfect sketch artist.

"Yes, you are. You have your own way, that's all. Will you do it?"

He peers at me, his gaze steady. Focused. I'm hopeful this is a good sign.

Finally, he offers me a wide smile. "I'd love to."

5

Charlie

I'm investigating Amelia Norris when my day goes to hell.

Everything started as planned. After staying up most of the night reviewing my notes, I came to the office this morning ready to take control of the situation and get to the bottom of how it's possible Ethan Havers isn't Ethan Havers.

I called BioBlocks, the lab he used and did a background inquiry. The manager I finally got through to explained their process in detail, e-mailed me a copy of their privacy practices for genetic testing, and assured me their procedures and regulations are of the highest standards and strictly followed. There can be no mix-up since they're double and triple checked.

Of course, she wouldn't divulge information about specific lab results, due to privacy issues, and I had no intention of sharing the name, since I'm trying to keep this on the down low for now, but the manager stated they'd be happy to redo the

DNA testing of my client and his parents with proper authorization.

My research came up with nothing damnable on the company either. BioBlocks is registered with the Better Business Bureau, has no complaints filed on them in the past three years of operation, and appears to be running a legit business for law enforcement and general consumers.

They've been in the news frequently since Carl used them for his news episode, and the social visibility has tripled their public clientele, even though they do not offer a database to build your family tree or connect you to those with your DNA. They are seen as more legitimate than online sources.

After striking out there, I called my source at Family Ties, the local DNA registry and ancestry company I use for clients. Much like the more popular online sites, they have a wide variety of services, including simple genetic tests and software to assist you in building your family tree. They also help connect you with genealogists like me who can create it for you and work with you to discover others in their system who might be related to you.

I ask if she knows of any instances where a child's DNA doesn't match his parents even with proof he is their son. She's seen and heard a lot and refers me to the well-known chimera cases I discussed with Ethan. On occasion, someone receives another person's stem cells or bone marrow, and that can screw up the findings. But those are rare, just like chimeras.

Time to attack the situation from the other end. If I have to go to Carl and Lily and tell them Ethan is not their biological son, I need to have a few ducks in a row to explain how this happened. I dive into Amelia and her background, wondering how my sister is doing on the age progression sketch I asked her for. I'm not sure if I want it to resemble him or not.

Amelia Norris was a whacko who somehow made it through the system. A nurse for many years, she suffered from bouts of depression and anxiety. My notes on her are sparse given that my team had no connection to her prior to her neighbor giving her up. A babysitter for the Havers—she had great recommendations they told us—she up and took off with the baby one day shortly after he was born. She changed her name, moved around frequently, and never enrolled him in school or took him for regular medical checkups and immunizations. By all accounts, she snatched him and disappeared like a ghost.

I dig into my various databases and look up information regarding her and her family before she became a kidnapper. Outside of some family alcoholism, there is little to be found. Medical records are not something I can access without a warrant, but I make notes on living relatives and several friends Amelia had so I can begin making calls and interviewing them in-depth about her.

I've hit two dead ends with family leads when Meg blows into the office and slaps down a sketch. "What do you think?" she asks.

I study the face in detail, and it's good, very well done. Something about it, though, lacks the usual Meg touch. Hers are so real; they look as if they'll come to life on the page. This one appears flat and...not like one of hers at all.

When she left the office this morning, she was tired and jittery. Her demeanor has changed now. She's relaxed and there's a spark in her eyes I haven't seen in a long time.

I sit back in my chair and cross my hands over my belly. "Maybe this was a bad idea. You're biased after all. You did the original age progression, and you've seen Ethan in person now at fifteen."

"Biased?" Her tone conveys affront, but the spark is still there.

There's something she's not telling me but I can't pinpoint

what it is. "It's subconscious. I know you don't mean to let confirmation bias slant your work, but in this case—"

"I didn't do the sketch for that very reason. I knew I couldn't be objective."

Now I know. "You went and saw your friend."

She nods. "Jerome did it. What do you think?"

I think that she needs to get laid, but she's not relaxed enough for that to have happened. She thinks her crush on Jerome is a secret. She also believes I don't know about the pot.

We all need our secrets. "It's not as good as yours would've been, but I appreciate the fact you had someone else sketch the progression. You never fail to amaze me."

A smile spreads across her face. "Looks just like him, doesn't it? The chin, the slant of the eyes, even the earlobes."

It *does*. I'm slightly relieved and irritated. I need an answer, something that points me in the right direction. This only seems to muddle things more in my mind.

"Jerome wouldn't take payment," she says. "He just wants to know how things turn out."

I eye her and feel my stomach bottom out. I tap the sketch. "You didn't tell him who this is, did you?"

"Not who he is specifically."

I close my eyes and rein in the sick feeling in my stomach. "We don't want this to get out to the media, Meg. The whole thing could become a public shitstorm before we've even secured the retests."

In the reception area, I hear the phone ring. We're still dealing with one hell of a media frenzy with the arrest of Billy Ray. Haley and I've been fielding calls all morning from the press wanting statements from both me and my sister, and I, personally, am not ready for another ugly brush with fame.

She waves a hand in the air as if shooing away my worries. "Jerome only knows Ethan's first name."

I wish I shared her confidence. I may have to call and threaten the guy.

"Charlie?" Haley buzzes me. "There's a kid on line one who claims he's a new client and needs to speak to Meg, but she's not picking up her office phone. Can you take it?"

My sister's eyes have that spark again. "How can he look so much like Carl and Lily's son but not be him?"

I tell Haley to send the call through and I put Ethan on speaker. "Hi, Ethan. What's up?"

"I got a hit!" He's out of breath, as if he's running. "I uploaded my DNA results to that database and I have a match! Looks like a third cousin. I'm heading home now to dive deeper."

"What database?"

Meg's brows wiggle slightly and she pulls her lips in, taking a step back toward the door.

"Stop," I tell her, coming out of my seat. She freezes, still pinching her lips between her teeth. What has she done? "What database?" I ask Ethan again, but really, I'm asking both.

I hear rustling and more heavy breathing. The kid is definitely running or riding his bike like a maniac. "The one Meg told me about last night. She said it could take weeks, but I already have a match! I'm on my way home to email the guy. Told the school I was sick."

I eye my sister and see her trying to hide a smile.

And failing.

"You told him about GenCo?" I hiss. The public website is free and allows people who don't want to pay mainstream online sites a yearly fee for services such as building family trees and hooking them up with potential genetic matches. I often send people who can't afford me there to look for matches.

"Sorry," she mouths, but I can see she isn't. She must've

figured he'd be tempted to bypass the age restriction and upload his test results. She was right.

I like things to be linear, calculated, and planned. I go from step A to step B and so on. Meg scatterguns the world and sees what falls out.

I close my eyes and feel my world spinning farther out of control. "We have to tell your parents," I say to Ethan. A demand, or command. If they find out before we've told them… "I'll call your dad and set up a meeting to explain everything and get new samples to confirm you're not their son."

"But my mom—"

I say goodbye and cut him off. There's no turning back or keeping things on the down low any more. I buzz Haley, ignoring Meg.

"Yes?" Haley says.

"Get me Jackie DelRay's number, would you? I need to make a call."

6

Meg

*C*harlie is pissed. I don't kid myself—or her—by acting like I didn't know this would happen. When investigating, she has a process. She ticks off all her little boxes and methodically moves forward. By slipping Ethan the GenCo information, I've done the equivalent of bulk-checking Charlie's boxes and moved right to phase ten.

We pull up the long, winding drive of Carl Havers' mansion. It's sandy brick and glowing white arches give it a regal look befitting a man whose spent the majority of his life in front of a camera. Everything in place and perfectly groomed.

Charlie pulls in and kills the engine. "Let me do the talking. Swear to God, Meg, if you speak, I might shoot you right in front of Carl and Lily."

I can't help the snort that pops out. "Hey, how many times should I apologize for the GenCo thing? I thought it'd help. And, excuse me, but it appears it did. We have a bonafide lead."

"I'll give you that, but I'd have preferred to gather some facts before having to tell the Havers I screwed up and gave them the wrong damned child back."

I stare at my sister's amazing cheekbones, the soft curves of her relaxed mouth and her all-around composed face. As good as she is at masking her emotions, I know her. I know what this work means to her, the need to bring answers—correct ones—to people in pain. It'd probably hurt less if I tied her to a stake over a raging fire. Guilt slams me and I shake my head. We're both in this for the correct reasons, but our methods are wildly different. Something Charlie is better at recognizing than I am.

"You're right. I didn't think of it like that. All I saw was a way to get to the finish line. I didn't anticipate the rubble left behind."

She reaches behind my seat and grabs her briefcase, yanking it through the opening between us. "What's done is done. Besides, we'd have gotten to this point anyway."

We exit the car with me doing a silent pinky swear to keep my mouth shut. I've already put Charlie in an awkward position and speaking out of turn will only make it worse.

Tick-a-lock. That's me.

Before we even ascend the slate steps, the front door opens and Carl greets us. He's wearing gray dress slacks and a periwinkle button down that enhances his chocolate eyes and black hair. Pair that with broad shoulders and this guy is a total stud. No wonder he's made millions as a television anchor.

"Agent Schock," he says, "hello."

"Good morning, Carl. Thank you for seeing us. And, it's Charlie. I'm not with the Bureau anymore."

The two shake hands, then Charlie turns to me, rests her hand on my arm. "You remember my sister, Meg. She's my partner at our agency."

We exchange greetings and like the rest of him, I find it a wholly pleasant experience. His palm is warm and there's an energy about him that puts me at ease. The man is a master. It's almost too much. The good looks, the calm energy.

Too perfect.

Too...intimidating.

But, I suppose that's the point.

He ushers us through the marble-floored foyer to a set of double doors just beyond dual winding staircases that create a wonderful focal point.

"We'll meet in my study. More privacy there."

"That's fine," Charlie says.

A housekeeper appears at the end of the hallway and Carl, the gracious host, requests a tray of beverages for us. At this point, I think my sister needs a gallon of vodka.

The study is not what I expect. Light, muted colors abound. No gleaming, rich woods here. It's all clean lines and modern furniture that gives the room a cool sixties vibe. The artist in me loves the unexpectedness of it.

Carl waves us to a sitting area with a sharp-edged light gray sofa and two curvy, wingback chairs. Carl takes one and leaves the sofa for us.

Before we even settle in, the housekeeper appears and sets a tray on the steel coffee table. The tray is filled with two carafes and a plate of tea cookies that look homemade. Realizing I've skipped lunch, my sweet tooth wants a nibble.

Carl holds one of the carafes up and Charlie nods. Personally, I don't think she needs coffee right now. Caffeine will only amp up her already fried nerves. But...*tick-a-lock.*

She's a big girl.

I decline and snatch a cookie. Anything to keep my mouth busy.

Carl sips his, deems it acceptable and places it on the table beside him. "So, ladies, what can I help you with?"

My sister sits tall, lifting her chin slightly. Her body

language is all business and I'm once again impressed by her ability to compartmentalize.

"Well," Charlie says, "I'm not sure you're aware of this, but Ethan paid us a visit yesterday."

Carl's eyebrows hitch a fraction. Beyond that, total deadpan. Between him and Charlie, it'd be a bloody battle for the Don't-Sweat-It award.

"My son?"

"Yes."

"Wow." Carl lets out a breath. "He's always been resourceful. Our own fault, I suppose. We've been forthright about his kidnapping. We couldn't have him finding details we hadn't given him. Over the years, we've shared only what we thought he could emotionally handle. Given his maturity, he knows most of it. Why would he come looking for you?"

"He tracked me down at the office and wanted to discuss the results of the DNA test the three of you did as part of his school project."

"Ah." His shoulders seem to release, but the movement is so small I could've imagined it. "He's been fascinated with that project. Given his history, I'm sure it's not unusual."

I eye my sister. Carl has given her the perfect segue so I sit back and wait for Charlie to do her magic.

"I'd imagine I'd feel the same if I were in his place." Charlie digs into her briefcase, pulls out a file and grabs several pages. "These are copies. Ethan gave them to me yesterday."

"Hang on. He brought *you* the results?"

Charlie holds the documents in mid-air, but Carl remains still. Human instinct is funny that way. It's as if he knows he shouldn't touch them, much less look.

I slide a sidelong glance at Charlie, who is still holding them out. Finally, she sets them on the coffee table and rests her hands in her lap. "Look, Carl, I don't know how to tell you this so I'm just going to say it. According to these, yours and Lily's DNA is not a match for Ethan."

His eyes shoot to me a second, as if I can help him unhear what he doesn't want to know. He whips back to Charlie, cocking his head and staring at her like she's suddenly grown five heads.

"What the hell are you talking about?"

The room goes silent as Carl's features start to collapse. Narrowed eyes, tight lips, shoulders flying back. It's all there. Battle posture.

As opposed to my sister who remains unmoving. Not a flinch, a shift of feet, a straightening of her spine. Nothing.

Frozen.

Tick-a-lock, tick-a-lock, tick-a-lock.

She'll kill me if I speak. Absolutely carve me up and bury my body where it'll never be found. I'm aware of this, yet, I know Charlie. My strong, independent, conscientious sister has just admitted to herself that she made a mistake that could wreck any number of lives.

And it's paralyzed her.

Tick-a-lock, tick-a-lock, tick-a-lock.

I can't. No way. Not with my best friend struggling. I'll take her wrath any day before I'll let her fail.

I lean forward and touch the top of the reports. It breaks the odd spell between them and he focuses on my hand, then meets my eye. "What is she talking about?"

"Mr. Havers," I say. "Ethan may not be your son."

7

Charlie

*T*hank God for Meg. My blunt, in-your-face, amazing sister. She's just saved me from speaking out loud the one thing I haven't fully admitted to myself.

Failure.

I hate it with a passion.

Both Carl and I shift our eyes to her. His voice is barely a croak. "What?"

I'm finally able to find my own voice, and although my emotions are churning, I stay calm and exude confidence. "Eight years ago when I returned Ethan, my team recommended you and Lily have his DNA tested to make sure it was a match. You refused."

His gaze, now tortured as a piece of reality sinks in, pins me with defiance. "You said that woman admitted he was our baby. We had that sketch."

"The evidence pointed to the child being yours," I agree. "But without DNA confirmation, there was always a chance it was wrong."

His body is suddenly primed with tension, ready to jump to his feet, but I see him clinging to his frozen countenance with determination. "You can't be serious."

There have been times in my life when I've had to deliver bad news, usually due to an unexpected tragedy or the discovery of a long buried secret. I've had to tell a few of my genealogy clients the father who raised them was not biologically theirs.

I received training for sticky situations like this in the FBI, but I find it woefully unhelpful at the moment. "Carl, I know this is a lot to take in, but we're going to get to the bottom of it. First, we need to retest your DNA, along with Lily and Ethan's. There is an outside possibility something was screwed up at the lab Ethan used and all of this is just a mistake."

He slumps back in his chair, the rigidity giving way to fear. He is totally still and silent for several long moments. "What are the odds of that?"

Like me, Carl is cerebral. He wants facts, percentages, reassurances. I'm sure as a news anchor and morning host, he has to be three steps ahead of everyone else mentally, his job requires it. He needs to be knowledgeable about his subject matter at all times, even when there's no cue card or electronic prompter available.

There is definitely no cue card or prompter for this.

I want to give him the easy solution, the one that'll give him hope, but in my opinion, false hope is worse than none. I don't lie to string people along or put off telling them bad news.

"The odds are very low," I admit, "but there's a possibility there *is* an alternate explanation why they don't match. I am exploring all angles. I *will* find an answer."

His dark eyes flash anger, hope, then the beginnings of devastation. His son means everything to him. The entire office is filled with pictures of Ethan through the years. Like any doting father, Carl has immortalized his son in Halloween costumes, his Little League uniform, the two of them at a hockey game sharing popcorn and big smiles. There's an Easter egg hunt, a birthday party, Ethan and his friends in the swimming pool out back.

My heart reels for him, and for Ethan as well. Carl, Lily, and this boy have created a family, whether they are related by blood or not.

A tense silence falls in the room. I feel Meg getting antsy and I shoot her a look. She's only spoken once, but it was a bomb, and while I wish she tempered her bluntness on occasion, I also want to thank her. She saved me from delivering the news, and now, she wants to save me again by comforting Carl as best as she can, reassuring both of us in a way that everything will be fine.

"Ethan is an amazing young man," Meg says, ignoring my warning glance. "You've raised him to feel safe and loved. That's what matters, regardless of what we discover."

Carl stares at her as if she's speaking another language. "If Ethan isn't mine, my son is still out there! Don't tell me what matters. Who knows what my real son has endured, what's happened to him."

Meg only nods.

Carl's eyes snap to me. "How could you let this happen? I mean, you've got to be kidding me, right?" He forms a fist and thumps it against his chest. "I feel it, right here. I know he's my son."

The emotion rolls off him, flooding over me, and I wish there was something I could say to make all of this okay, but there isn't. I pull out a consent form from my briefcase, and lay it on the results. "If you will sign this, I'll help you with the new testing kit to get a fresh sample."

The emotion drains out of him as fast as it came. He shakes his head, rolls his eyes, and looks out the window to his left. "I can't believe this. I just can't."

Meg and I sit still, giving him time to process. Behind us, the office door opens and Ethan sticks his head in. "Dad?"

When Carl's gaze falls on the boy, his eyes tear. He waves Ethan in.

Ethan says "hi" to Meg and I and we acknowledge him silently.

"Everything okay?" His attention darts between the three of us.

I reassure him with a nod and go into client/investigator mode. "We were discussing the genetic results with your father." I emphasize "father," knowing it may be a sore point at the moment, but it seems important. Biology or not, they are bonded. "I know you two have a lot to discuss, and we'll get out of your hair as soon as I get the samples and new consent."

I pull two DNA kits out of my briefcase and set them on the table. Carl stares at them as if they might be lions ready to pounce.

Ethan snatches one up, eager. "No problem." He hands it to Carl before grabbing the second for himself. "Come on, Dad. Let's do this."

It's almost as if they've reversed roles, Ethan becoming the adult and offering guidance to Carl. Beleaguered, he rises, accepts the kit, and starts to follow Ethan from the room.

I breathe a heavy sigh of relief.

It's short lived. The door flies open once more and in rushes Lily. She is a stunning beauty with long, auburn hair, porcelain skin, and sparkling green eyes.

"Ethan?" The heavily lined eyes take all of us in at once, but her focus lights on her son. She goes to him, brushing his bangs to the side. "The school called and said you were sick. What's wrong?"

Her attention slides to the test kits, then to Meg and I, a frown creasing her forehead. A brief flicker of recognition passes over her expression when she sees me, then I think I see the tiniest hint of fear.

Carl, who stiffened the moment she marched in, motions at me. "Lily, you remember Agent Schock."

"It's just Dr. Schock now," I correct. "I'm no longer with the FBI."

Before she can respond, Ethan channels Meg, dropping the bomb about everything. He tells his mother the truth about why he left school, why Meg and I are there, and why he and Carl are about to take another DNA test.

With each revelation, she steps back—*bam, bam, bam*—Ethan's words like physical blows. Horror floods her perfect face.

When he finishes, Lily sinks into the chair Carl vacated, the sparkling eyes now haunted. The smiling face from TV is contorted into confusion, full-blown fear lurking in the tiny crow's feet, now evident.

After a minute, she shakes her head like she's awakening from a bad dream. She sits forward, placing her elbows on her knees and clasping her hands as she looks at me. "Agent Schock," she implores, "what is this nonsense? Is this some sick joke?"

Lily hails from the south and has a soft accent and good manners. Her on-camera persona is one of Southern charm and politeness. Everything is schooled into model-perfect control—head up, chin forward, every pore oozing charisma. Her teeth are as white as the scarf artfully slung around her neck. She smiles now, as if I'm about to reveal this is a prank, her eyes encouraging me to tell her none of this is real.

What can I say? "I'm sorry, Mrs. Havers. It's not."

Shock is a funny thing, and I see another bout of denial, fear, and rejection play tag across her features.

Her focus shifts to Ethan. "I don't remember anything about this biology project. I never gave you permission to do a DNA test."

"You were out of town that week," he replies. "It was just Dad and I. He signed the slip."

Carl offers more explanation, as if Lily's whereabouts during that time period might clarify everything. "You were on location doing the Good Morning Atlanta segment, remember?"

Her eyes narrow ever so slightly, her glare a polar ice cap. "Well, it certainly would've been nice if someone had let me in on this. You are something else, Carl. He's my son, too. As usual, you did it your way."

Carl jerks his head in my direction then levels his own scathing glance at his wife. "We'll talk about it later."

America's sweethearts indeed.

"Oh, we will," she says then turns to me again. "I find it absolutely ridiculous there's any question about his DNA, and I never would've agreed to this project."

I hand the results to her. "Regardless, we have to either confirm or refute these."

She glances down, but doesn't take them. I return them to the table and withdraw the third kit. "The only thing we can do at this point is move forward. I need all three of you to retake the test and I will run them through the lab I use for investigation purposes. Once we have confirmation, we can proceed. My sister and I will handle this personally, and we will put all available resources into finding the truth."

Lily glances at Meg, back to me. She sets her jaw, notices the sketch. Her face softens.

"My sister and I run a private investigation service, and we will handle this at no charge to you, of course," I continue. "Meg did the original age progression on Ethan, but that"—I point to the one Lily is staring at—"was done yesterday by another qualified—and unbiased—sketch artist who's never met him."

She shakes her head adamantly. "I'm sorry, but I don't believe any of this. You had proof Ethan was ours when you brought him to us. What do you hope to prove by this little stunt?"

She's hanging on to denial pretty hard. Not that I expected less, but even the cold hard facts of the analyses seem to be lost on her.

She snatches up the sketch, rises to her full height, and shoves it in my face. "This is my son, I don't care what you say, and I think it's time you leave. Be assured, the second you step out of my home, I'll call my lawyer. I'm reporting you to the FBI, whether you work for them or not. Did you pull some ridiculous stunt like this and get yourself fired?"

The soft-spoken accent is still there, even if the politeness is gone. I'd be the same way if I was told Meg wasn't my sister, or if my mom and dad weren't my biological parents. Luckily, I've had some experience helping people handle revelations about their families.

I use my most soothing tone. "I know this is a terrible thing to consider, Lily. I feel horrible about what happened, but we have to redo these and be sure."

She hugs the sketch to her generous breasts and a tear slips from one of her eyes down her cheek. "I don't care what any results say." She looks at Ethan and Carl, her lower lip trembling. "He is mine and you can take your tests with you when you leave."

"But, mom—" Ethan starts toward her and she holds up the hand, a stop sign.

"Get out of my house," she says to me and Meg. Her voice is still sugary and genteel, even though there's steel underneath. She punctuates her next statement with an artificial smile. "And if you breathe a word of this to anyone, I will sue you for everything you're worth."

8

Meg

$\mathcal{J}$t's ten in the morning and I'm in my office aligning a prosthetic brown eye in my latest reconstruction when my sister bellows my name.

"Conference room! Matt! You, too."

A meeting. Excellent. At this point, I can't even guess what this might be. After being tossed out of the Havers' two days earlier, we've heard zip from Ethan and my sister is on a tear.

Matt has spent the last forty-eight hours trying to avoid her. Me? I'm not so lucky. I live next door and after the lecture I got last night about proper garbage placement, I'm half-tempted to call JJ and tell him to get his fine self over there tonight and give her an orgasm. Maybe ten. Whatever it takes.

The man is a civil servant, after all.

"Meg!" Charlie screams.

Crap. "Hey! I'm in the middle of putting an eye in. Can you give me a second?"

Without a doubt, I'll need meditation after this.

I set it, give it a quick study. "I'll be back, Fred. Sit tight."

Yes, I talk to the skulls.

Sue me.

I leave Fred and make my way to the conference room where Charlie has spread a bunch of files out. She's pushed three chairs against the wall, something she does when she wants freedom to slide back and forth behind the table. She's currently arranging the files in some sort of order while Matt watches.

His arms are crossed and he meets my gaze with a she's-bonkers look.

After this, I'm putting the emperor on speed dial.

For now, I lightly knock on the table. "What's this?"

Charlie doesn't bother to look up. "Everything on my old laptop regarding the kidnapping."

"Uh," Matt says, "should you even have these?"

"They're my personal notes. Call it my diary. Besides, are you gonna tell?"

"A little reminder," I begin, "his fiancé works for the Bureau. Did you stop to think you might be putting him in an awkward position with Taylor?"

Charlie finally glances at me. Her lips are pressed into a hard line. Yep, I'm starting to piss her off.

Ask me if I care?

When it comes to cases, my sister is indomitable. I admire that in her, but there are times she pushes too hard. Sometimes, she needs to be saved from herself.

She slowly shakes her head.

Yeah, definitely pissing her off.

"Okay." She swings to Matt. "Am I putting you in a tough spot with Taylor?"

"As long as I don't have to lie to her, no."

"You don't have to. Feel free to tell her we're reviewing my personal notes on the case." She passes Matt a folder. "Witness statements. You start with these." She picks up another, hands it to me. "I know you're busy, but I need fresh eyes. Can you help?"

How am I supposed to resist when she asked so nicely? I let out a small sigh. "Yes, but." I pause to gather my thoughts. My sister doesn't like to be coddled or patronized so I have to choose my words carefully.

"What?"

"I'm worried about you. You're too close to this."

"Of course I am. It was my case and I blew it. Two families could be destroyed. What am I supposed to do? Walk away?"

I don't know. I'm not about to say that, but my silence has already told her I have no idea how to answer.

The folder is still in her hand and I grasp it. "What is this?"

"Hate mail to Carl and Lily. Letters, emails, anything they received in the months leading up to Ethan's birth. There might be something of interest."

I slide into one of the chairs on my side and flip it open. The first document is what appears to be a photocopy of a type-written letter. Behind it is another—this one definitely a copy. It's a paste-up of magazine letters. So much for this being Charlie's personal diary.

No wonder she gave me this. This is the one she shouldn't have. Matt's folder? Those are her personal notes that hopefully won't get him in trouble with Taylor. I don't know, the whole thing seems to be riding the edge of ethical. Never mind legal.

An hour later, I have three stacks in front of me. The first being general nasty-grams. Run of the mill stuff. Carl's hair wasn't right, his suits too tight, skin too shiny. Lily didn't fare much better. She had ugly lipstick, watermelon breasts, and the insult of all insults, she looked fat.

As if a pregnant woman should be thin?

The second pile contained anything with the potential for

violence and the third, full out, no-doubt-about-it physical threats.

These were the worst. Psychos who'd taken the time to let Lily know they'd cut her baby from the womb then sever her head. Or, to Carl, that they'd rape his pregnant wife and make him watch.

Sick, sick, sick.

I don't know how Charlie did this job. I've been at it fifty-nine minutes and my heart chakra is already blown.

The alarm system beeps. Someone has entered via the front.

A distraction. *Thank you, thank you.*

Who it could be, I have no idea, since all deliveries tend to come to the back door. Right now, I don't care. It gives me an excuse to leave Charlie's house of horrors.

"I'll see who that is."

"Haley is there," Charlie says.

"I'm aware, but I need a break."

"Oh. Sorry. If you're tired—"

"I'm fine. I just...need a break."

A second later, Taylor glides through the door pulling a cart loaded with two banker's boxes. She's wearing a cream pantsuit and taupe heels. Her long blond hair is pulled into a sleek ponytail and she looks like the polished professional she is.

A smile lights Matt's face as he rises from the chair at the end of the table. "Aren't you a sight for sore eyes?"

They share a quick kiss which screams of affection and reminds me just how lacking my personal life is.

I look down at my hands, picking at a smidge of clay stuck under my nails.

"Ladies," Taylor says, "sorry to interrupt your day, but I come bearing gifts."

From her seat across from me, Charlie closes her eyes and

slaps her hands together in prayer. "Please tell me those are copies of the Havers' FBI files."

Charlie opens her eyes and Taylor jerks her head once. "These are copies of the Havers' FBI files. You can thank me later."

"Shit," Matt said. "Babe, what are you doing?"

"I'm smuggling copies from headquarters."

So much for putting Matt in an awkward position.

Across from me, Charlie is on the move, swinging around the table. "Oh, my God, Taylor. I love you."

"You'd better. I just spent two days taking pictures of this stuff and using my home printer to make these. I also moved the files to a thumb drive for you. If I get caught, my career is over."

"Charlie," Matt says, "don't touch those." He locks his gaze on Taylor. "You can't do this. Not for me."

"Sure I can. I love you and this case is tearing you up. If I can help, I'm going to. I don't care what it costs me."

"Blah, blah," Charlie, the master of sensitivity states. "Can I look? Pretty please?"

Taylor nods at Matt. "I'm good. Honestly. Besides, a certain investigator, namely you, from Schock Investigations helped me find my sister. Consider it repayment of a favor."

Charlie smacks her hands together. "Good enough for me."

Poor Matt. Between Charlie and Taylor, he'll never win this. Finally, he relents, bending to grab the boxes and set them on the table, flipping the lids off.

Charlie, being Charlie, hooks a hand around the edge of one and yanks it toward her. "What did you bring us?"

"Anything I thought was relevant. Witnesses, possible suspects, hospital employees. Addresses, numbers. Everything I thought might help."

Charlie's jaw drops. Without a doubt, Taylor has just saved us a ton of digging. She's also put her tail on the line.

"Taylor, I..." Charlie meets the other investigator's eyes. "I don't know what to say. This is amazing. Thank you."

She waves Charlie's comment away. "Don't sweat it. You and I? We're the same animal. We want justice. Always. And if this happened to me, I'd go insane. Let's just figure out what the hell happened."

Another beep sounds—front door—and Charlie meets my eye. Who the hell was this now? Thirty seconds later, the Emperor of Cold Cases appears in the hallway. Like Taylor, he's dressed for work, looking sharp in a black suit and gray shirt. His gaze swings from Charlie to Matt to Taylor then me.

"A party," he says. "And I wasn't invited?"

The smile he offers is electric, playful even, so I swivel from him back to my sister. With a lead-in like that, Charlie is bound to fire back with something witty.

Except...nothing. She sits there, staring. Her jaw is relaxed, her lips soft. If she was mad, I'd know it. This isn't anger.

What I'm not seeing is a smile so this sure isn't happiness either.

Honestly, I don't know what this is. A buzz shoots straight up my neck as silence builds like a funnel cloud about to take out a town.

I spin my chair back to the emperor. "JJ, come in. We'll update you."

His smile is still in place, his features composed. Relaxed even. But something is...off. This is that of a career prosecutor who knows how to play a jury. Even when blindsided.

"Meg," Charlie says.

The way she drags out my name, *Meeggg*, leads me to believe I've screwed up.

Royally.

Could it be that she hasn't told JJ about Ethan? Seriously? The man is a genius at solving cold cases. More than that, he's a tireless victims' advocate.

So, right now, I couldn't give a crap my sister is irritated with me. JJ's office should be involved.

No question.

"You didn't tell him," I say.

It comes out as the accusation it is and I receive the Charlie death glare.

"No," JJ answers, his voice even. "I don't believe she's told me."

"You have to."

"I do *now*. JJ, come to my office."

Still filleting me with her laser focus stare, she pushes out of her chair and storms around the table.

"Hey," I say, "You can death-glare me all you want. *You* screwed this one up. Not me."

JJ stands to the side as Charlie moves past. If he knows anything about my sister, it's to get out of her way when she's on a roll.

"Well," he observes as he watches her go. "This should be good."

9

Charlie

I'm shaking so hard, I nearly twist my ankle walking to my office. Stomping, is more like it. I'm angry, yes. Not at Meg, but at myself.

I'm too wired to sit, too apprehensive to look at JJ. I pace behind the desk, nearly twist my ankle again, and kick off the offending shoes. They smack the wall like bullets—*whack, whack*.

Without the four-inch heels, I can pace faster, but I'm now that much shorter than JJ.

"Hey," he says, his voice like melted butter. "What's going on?"

The real reason I'm shaking—the underlying emotion causing my anger—is fear. JJ should've been the first person I reached out to. He has as much at stake in the outcome of this situation as I do.

The thing I suck at is admitting mistakes. The one person I

never want to admit I screwed up to is the dark haired man watching me with his intense eyes.

"I'm looking into an old case," I tell him, avoiding those eyes and flipping through some files on my desk. "At the time it was closed, I thought I did everything right, but now…"

I can't bring myself to say it. Why didn't I insist Carl and Lily have that damn DNA test when I returned Ethan? I've asked myself that a hundred times the last couple days. Yes, I tried, but I should've pushed harder to get them to consent, or my superior, a judge, *somebody*, to force them to do it.

JJ is still standing across from me, looking slightly confused. "I take it since Taylor's here, this has to do with an FBI investigation?"

"You never saw her, okay? At the moment, everything's off the books. There is no official reopening of this case. Not yet, anyway, but I have to get to the bottom of this, and be ready for the backlash that could happen."

He nods sympathetically, but is still lost as to what I'm talking about. "And you didn't tell me because…? Do I need some kind of deniability about what you're investigating?"

JJ was an assistant U.S. attorney doing grunt work when Ethan was kidnapped. That's how we met—working the case. He was part of the team tasked with finding the kidnapper and bringing him or her to justice. I fell for JJ over a late-night session in an FBI conference room, files strewn over the table, half-empty coffee cups lined up like a centerpiece, enough sexual tension to make it hard to breathe. Both of us were exhausted, but determined.

I remember these same sexy eyes of his looking at me with a mixture of admiration and respect. It was the biggest turn-on of my life. I could see his star rising like a comet. I felt his power even then.

I look at him now and see the same determination—to help me, whatever the problem. This is also sexy, even though there's nothing he can do, and I'm hellbent not to admit I need it.

"There's nothing you can do to change what happened then, and I'll minimize any collateral damage that might fall your way. I didn't tell you about it because the blame is on me, and I'm trying to find a way to fix it."

That's the truth. Unfortunately, his career is on the line same as mine. The details, the facts, will make no difference if —*when*—I go public.

Because I'll have to eventually. Last night when I couldn't sleep and lay in bed tossing and turning, worrying about Carl and Lily sharing this, I realized, they may actually do the opposite. Whether they go through with a second genetic test and analysis, Lily will try to bury the results. She made that clear at our meeting. It's been nothing but crickets, total silence, since.

But if Ethan *isn't* theirs, he belongs to someone else. The real Havers' child is potentially out there somewhere. He deserves to be returned to his biological parents.

Meaning, that no matter what Carl and Lily do or don't do, I'll have to investigate, find the truth, and reveal it.

JJ takes a step toward the desk, toward me. "I think you better tell me what's going on." He reaches to take my hand, stopping it as it rifles through files. "This isn't like you."

He's right. I hate the trepidation and dread coursing through my veins. I've been in plenty of unnerving situations over the years, and I never give into the fear. But this? This is somehow different than staring down a serial killer or trying to out-think a terrorist. I'm facing myself.

His hand is warm, strong, as it holds mine. I stare into his gaze and feel myself stop shaking. He smiles at me and I can breathe again. My pulse slows, my shoulders relax. For a long moment, I feel like the old me, the take-no-prisoners Charlie who can handle anything.

That's what he does for me. Like Meg, he believes in me,

believes I'm the woman he fell for eight years ago over cold coffee and a missing child. He once told me that no matter what, he would always bet on me.

Too bad he was already married. Too bad he still is.

Maybe it's a good thing he *is*. How awkward if we were in a public relationship when the news breaks about Ethan.

I'm about to tell him what's going on when my phone buzzes. Haley comes over the speaker. "Jackleen DelRay on line one, returning your call, Charlie."

JJ's brow furrows. "The lawyer?"

I respond to Haley, "Tell her I'll call right back."

"You got it," she says.

JJ rubs the top of my hand with his thumb. "Tell me you're setting up a lunch date. That this doesn't have anything to do with this case you're diving back into."

Out front, I hear the door beep. Haley's voice is muffled as she greets whoever entered. Do we have an appointment this afternoon?

I withdraw my hand from JJ's grasp and take a deep breath, searching for the words to explain the predicament. "Jackie is my lawyer, in the event I need one. Which is likely."

The bushy brows rise again slowly. "Is it that bad?" he asks softly.

"It might be," I confess. "Do you remember the first case we worked together?"

His gaze scans my face and I see the wheels turning as he searches his memory. "The kidnapping case with that morning show host?"

"Carl Havers and his wife, Lily."

"What about them?"

"Their son..." I clasp my hands and twist my fingers. "All the evidence pointed to him being Ethan, but the kid, who's fifteen now, recently took a DNA test."

I see the handsome face of the man I love pale. His eyes go

flat, hard, as if he's guessed what I'm about to tell him. "You've got to be kidding. You don't mean—"

Before I have the chance to confirm it—as if we've somehow conjured one of the most important players in the case—a man appears in the doorway of my office.

"I tried to stop him," Haley says, peeking over the man's shoulder. "Sorry, Charlie."

Sorry, Charlie. Like the old tuna fish commercial. "It's okay," I tell her, my bold self-confidence failing me once again as I see the look on my visitor's face.

"They don't match," Carl says, ignoring JJ. His lips tremble and then he sets his jaw, clenches his fist as if he wants to punch me. His voice rises. "Ethan and I took new tests. They don't *goddamn* match!"

He must've ignored Lily's proclamation. Good for him.

"JJ, you remember Carl Havers." I round up my shoes and slide them back on, ready to do battle. "Why don't you come in and have a seat, Carl?"

Both men stare at me as if I've grown two heads. They're angry, perplexed, anticipating the worst. I don't have time for dread or fear now. I have to take control and do what I do best.

Solve the problem.

"Okay," I say, straightening my suit jacket with a little tug. "Ethan is not your son. Let's figure out whose son he is and bring home yours while we're at it."

I sound like I've got my shit together. Inside, I'm a hot mess. I look to JJ, hoping he'll put aside his shock and irritation, and jump onboard to help Carl.

"Bring home his son?" JJ taps a fist on my desk as if trying to bring me out of a dream—*rap, rap, rap.* "Did you seriously just say that?"

He appears appalled at my matter of fact tone. It's the best I could do, trying to instill confidence in Carl, and myself. "We have a problem, I'm trying to solve it."

His eyes are lit with anger. "One you left me out of the loop on? This could affect my career, too, you know. When exactly were you going to tell me, Charlize?"

The expression he gives me suggests it might affect our relationship as well. Trust is an issue for each of us. "I was about to explain everything to you. I'm well aware of the consequences this unfortunate event places all of us in."

His stare feels like he's stripping my soul, a dozen questions in his eyes. "I swear, you..."

JJ shakes his head as if he can't wrap his head around me not telling him. Everything is spinning out of control and I grab the desk, holding on.

I'm sorry, I want to say, and would if an angry Carl Havers wasn't standing here.

Carl clears his throat, demanding my attention. I ignore him, keeping my eyes on JJ.

I swear I can see the wheels spinning. The damage my silence has done is a jagged tear between us.

Then my rock steps back, turns on his heel and does the one thing I don't expect.

JJ walks out on me.

10

Meg

*B*y the time I get to the conference room door, JJ is striding down the hall. All I see are his straight posture and wide shoulders brutally pinned back. He marches by Haley, offering a quick nod, but not a word.

I don't know him that well. I've watched him do his magic in court, slinging his charm and brilliant smile like a master while jurors and witnesses sit enthralled. He's good. Really good.

And when he squares off with my formidable sister? Gosh, that's fun to see.

In all of that, I'm not sure I've ever seen him truly, blood-boiling angry.

At least until this moment. One thing I know is he's never left this office without at least a wave in my direction.

Whatever Charlie was thinking in not looping JJ in, I hope she can live with the ramifications. She loves this man. She may not have said it aloud or even admitted it to herself, but I know her and when she looks at him there's a happy softness that's reserved only for JJ.

Damn, Charlie and her pride.

Just as JJ swings out the front door Charlie steps into the hallway with Carl on her heels. She meets my gaze then jerks her head toward the conference room. If I thought she was pissed a few minutes ago, I don't dare open my mouth now.

I step back and wave them through. As he passes, Carl stares straight ahead. The skin on his carved cheekbones is firm, but not tight. Years of honing his craft at the anchor desk have made him an ace at neutrality.

I'm surrounded by people who hide their emotions for a living. It must be exhausting.

I follow behind them, avoiding the chairs by leaning against the wall.

Charlie stands at the head of the table. "Matt, Taylor, this is Carl Havers. Ethan's father."

From where I'm standing, all I can see is Carl's back and the twitch that followed Charlie's introduction. For the first time, his composure seems to slip and who could blame him? The man has raised a son who, based on the yelling we just heard, isn't his.

"Carl, this is Matt Stephens and Special Agent Taylor Sinclair from the FBI."

Carl whips his head in Charlie's direction. "FBI? Who gave you the right—"

"They didn't call me, sir. Matt and I are...involved. I offered to help."

Charlie gestures to the empty chair in front of Carl and he sits. "Taylor runs the cold case unit for the FBI. She's a friend and here in an unofficial capacity, as a favor to us."

"Fine. I need answers. Where the hell is my child? You gave

us the wrong goddamned kid back! What kind of idiot gets that wrong?"

Oh, ouch. A sharp stab pierces my chest and I steal a glance at Charlie, standing at the end of the table, head high and taking Carl's wrath. She may be built for this, but it's not altogether fair.

Before I think too hard about it, I move closer and tap a finger on the table. All heads swing to me. "Carl, this has to be devastating."

"Goddamn right it is. And don't defend her."

Oh, now he's pushing it. "*Her?* At the time of your son's kidnapping, Charlie was one member of an entire team. The *FBI* led this investigation. Don't you *dare* lay this on Charlie. She worked tirelessly for you and doesn't deserve to be your punching bag. I assure you, she feels bad enough."

"Meg." Charlie touches my arm. "It's all right."

Ha! My ass. "Uh, *no*. It's not. We're *helping* him. And he doesn't get to call you, or anyone here, names. Anger is one thing, but that's unacceptable. I don't care who he is."

By now, Carl, clearly unaccustomed to a solid set-down, is fuming. The color of his face has moved well past red. He's in eggplant territory now, leaving me to wonder if I've, as usual, gotten too impulsive.

But...oh well.

My sister may have screwed up with JJ, but Carl doesn't get to abuse her.

No.

Way.

Taylor rises from her chair and holds her hands up. "Let's all take a breath, okay? Mr. Havers, have a seat. Let's talk a few minutes."

"I can't talk to the FBI. My wife doesn't even know yet."

Taylor sets her hand on the table and leans in. "Right now, I'm simply a friend who happens to work for the

Bureau. I do think, however, if you've confirmed Ethan is not..."

The room goes silent. No need to actually state the obvious.

"He's not ours," Carl finally says, his voice barely a whisper. "I got the results this morning. Lily didn't want to do the test, but I sent mine and Ethan's out. I didn't tell her. I had to know."

Taylor offers a perfunctory nod. "In that case, I think it's time to bring in the FBI and find your biological child."

Beside me, Charlie eases out a breath. This has to be killing her. The last thing she wanted was for this to go public. We'd all hoped, Charlie more than anyone, the test had been wrong.

Carl peers up at Charlie, his eyes still too hard—accusatory —for my taste, but given the circumstances, I'll give him some slack.

"I don't want to put Ethan and Lily through an investigation like that."

For the first time, a bit of Charlie's composure slips and her shoulders collapse. Damn that JJ for walking out. We could use him about now. Not only for legal advice, but to shore Charlie up.

It takes all of three seconds for my sister to realize her armor has failed and she straightens, tilting her chin up as she goes. "I understand. But, Ethan is a smart kid. He came to us with this. Before long, he'll ask about the results. It might be best to tell him and Lily so we can move forward. And, Carl, I can't tell you how sorry I am."

The man shakes his head, then scrubs his hands over his face. "I can't believe this."

"It's a lot to absorb," Taylor says, her voice gentle and carrying a soft comfort she's probably had too much practice with. "You're probably in shock."

"I definitely am." He stands and faces Charlie. "I apologize for what I said. I'm...angry."

Charlie comes to her feet as well and holds both hands up.

"I appreciate that. Thank you. No offense taken." She takes a deep breath and seems to grow a little taller. "I really do want to help. If you'll allow us to keep working with you, I'll do it pro-bono. This is personal for me. I'd like the chance to find your child."

"That'll be my job," Taylor states. "You and Meg need to find Ethan's real parents. Can you do that?"

"He's already found a biological match," Charlie says. "A cousin. We'll start there."

11

Charlie

The next day, I feel both relieved and ready to crawl out of my skin.

Taylor is now reopening the official FBI case—it couldn't be in better hands—and she plans to schedule a small press conference as soon as they have a solid lead on where the real Havers' child is. Until then, she'll keep Carl, Lily, and Ethan mum on the situation.

The upper echelon at the Bureau has frozen me out and tried to take the case away from Taylor since she's involved with my employee, but someone—JJ probably—specifically requested her as lead investigator.

Meanwhile, Meg and Matt are working with me to figure out who Ethan belongs to. Since his underage status puts his account in jeopardy at GenCo, I'm trying to get ahead of it and put Carl in touch with the owners of the site to correct the issue before we contact the cousin.

I've managed to track down Cora Drummond, a woman who knew our kidnapper fifteen years ago, and have an appointment to interview her at three. I'm hoping she'll give me insight into Amelia Norris and why she abducted a baby. Since Ethan isn't the child she stole from Carl and Lily, I suspect he wasn't the first or only victim.

The fact she claimed he belonged to them before killing herself confuses me—did she suffer from mental illness, even though my notes on the case don't mention it?

I keep asking myself, what if she wasn't mentally ill? What if she honestly believed the baby she had *was* Ethan Havers? Where did the mix-up occur? Was she babysitting more than one kid that day when she made the decision to run away with him?

I've asked Taylor to round up a list of other missing children who fit the parameters around that timeframe in the three-state area, but with her current workload, it could be days before she gets to it. If JJ were speaking to me, I would've had him pressure the FBI to cough it up sooner. He's not, damn him, so I have to be patient.

I can't believe he walked out on me, no matter how pissed he might've been. Meg says I should call and apologize, and I should, but the fact is, if I had to do it all over again, I wouldn't change the way I handled the situation.

There was no point bringing him onboard until I had all the facts, which I didn't until Carl showed up and confirmed Ethan wasn't his. There was nothing JJ could've done before that was verified, and I'm not one to dump my shit in someone else's lap just to make myself feel better.

Meg wants me to talk about my feelings in regard to all of this—both Ethan and JJ—or she claims I'll explode. Implode is more like it. My muscles, my bones, my very tissues feel like they're pressing in on me.

I can't talk about feelings. I try, but I seem to be missing that gene. My tongue gets tied, and I start itching every time I have to admit I screwed up, that I'm a failure on so many levels, most especially in the relationship department.

What I *can* do is relieve the pressure inside me by pumping bullets into targets. My Smith & Wesson is getting a workout as I run and dodge imaginary enemies at the gun range.

Standing in a lane for target practice didn't suit—I needed to move, to get the adrenaline pumping and clear my head. Besides, standing still during an actual firefight will get you killed. I've always preferred practicing as if it's real life.

I duck, roll, and come up on one knee. *Bam, bam, bam.* Satisfaction courses through my veins along with the adrenaline.

Before I meet with Cora, I want to read my notes on Lily's interview again, and dig deeper into Norris's life at that time. She was a loner from all accounts, and it wasn't like she had to break into the Havers' home to steal the baby, but she may have had help.

If it was premeditated, she would've needed to purchase items for him, arrange for new identities for both of them, and figure out where she was going to take him. Did she plan to keep him all along, or sell him on the black market? These are the questions that plague me.

Bam, bam, bam. I hit another center mass, shift behind a half-wall for cover, and reload. Lily was a small-time news reporter prior to dating Carl and got pregnant before they married. The marriage and subsequent pregnancy brought her immense fame, fans of the couple eating up their fairytale romance and garnering her an equal amount of prestige. Their wedding was a huge event, as if they were American royalty. I never follow that stuff, but Meg eats it up.

Seven months along, Lily accepted a TV anchor position with the same network as Carl's morning show. She was a regular guest on that show, and often filled in for Carl's female anchor when she was sick or on vacation. By the time Ethan was born, the network decided Lily's fanbase was big enough to offer her a coveted slot—the home and family segment.

She and Carl were living the American dream... until it came crashing down, thanks to Amelia Norris.

I finish my target practice and clean my gun. My mind is clearer, my body a bit more relaxed. I toy with my phone as I'm leaving the range, silently trying out different ways of apologizing to JJ. Even though I wouldn't do things differently, I understand why he's angry. It's as much personal as it is professional.

I can at least take the first step to make amends and pray that between Taylor, the FBI, and myself, we figure out the truth before JJ's name gets dragged through the mud. Once news gets out, my reputation will take a beating for sure. I'm ready for it, but I don't want him to go down in flames with me.

I leave the locker room, phone still in hand when it rings. It's Meg.

"Where are you?"

I nod at the guy manning the front desk, and he gives me a salute. "Just leaving the range. What's up?"

"We have a problem, or more specifically, you and Taylor do."

I push through the double doors out into the murky sunshine. I'm still feeling good after my workout, but I'm instantly on alert. "What happened?"

"Lily Havers. Apparently, she's none too happy about reopening the case."

In the parking lot, I see two news vans. Outside each stands a reporter—one male and one female. The woman is fussing over her hair; her male counterpart straightens his tie, both holding microphones. Camera guys check their equipment.

"There she is," someone shouts, and everyone starts toward me.

"Shit."

"I know," Meg says. "It gets worse."

It's about to, all right. There's no way I can get to my car without going straight through the reporters rushing me and yelling questions, accusations.

I lift my chin and start walking as though I have blinders on and can't hear them.

I have to turn up the volume on my phone to hear Meg over their chaos. "She put out a complete media package—Twitter, Facebook, a video on YouTube, you name it. She's called a press conference that's to take place in a couple minutes, so you might want to get to a television. She claims she's suing you and the FBI."

I knew it was coming, and yet, it still feels like a slap across the face.

"What do you think of Lily Havers' accusations?" The male reporter shoves a microphone in my face as he and his cohorts keep pace with me. "Did you screw up, Dr. Schock? Did you give Carl and Lily the wrong child?"

The female reporter's microphone vies for my attention, practically knocking her competitor's away. "How could you make such a tragic mistake?" she yells at me as I fight my way to my car. "How could you do this to that family?"

"Charlie?" Meg calls from the phone. "What's going on?"

From a dark SUV a lane over from my vehicle, another woman emerges, hair swept back in a bun, power suit firmly in place. She marches toward me, her face set for battle. "My client has no comment at this time."

"I have to call you back." I end the conversation and slip the phone into my pocket.

Jackie DelRay comes in like a firestorm, and before I know it, both reporters are backing away as she threatens them with lawsuits, and more indirectly, with physical bodily harm if they so much as look at me wrong.

She does it all with a smile as she hustles me into my vehicle. "I'll handle this. Meet me at your office in twenty minutes. Don't talk to anyone in between."

She shuts the door on my reply, and for a moment, I watch and admire her as she backs the reporters all the way up to their vans. They are packing up to leave as I hurry out of the parking lot. I wonder if they'll try to follow me to Schock Investigations, but whatever Jackie said to them does the trick.

No one follows me but her.

12

Meg

I hang up with Charlie and cluck my tongue. "The shit hit the fan already."

Leaning on his car beside me, Matt cocks his head. "What'd I miss?"

"It sounds like the press is all over Charlie. They somehow tracked her down. I think I heard something about a client having no comment. Hopefully, that was Jackie doing her thing."

Matt lets out a low whistle. "Oh, man. Those reporters better watch their asses. DelRay'll eat them for breakfast then feed the leftovers to wolves."

We once assisted on a homicide case involving one of Taylor's friends and subordinates. Jackie had been the defense attorney, and I learned fairly quickly that the woman was a force who knew criminal law inside and out.

She and Charlie together? Unbeatable. No doubt.

I tuck my phone in my purse and gesture to the early nineteen hundreds style bungalow in front of us. The grass is half-dead and the sagging porch manages to hold four flower pots with drooping plants. My artist's eye zooms to the white clay pot missing a hunk of the lip and I instantly want to sketch it. Why, I'm not sure. Maybe because the really interesting parts of life lie in the imperfect.

I bring my attention back to Matt. "This is the cousin's house?"

"Hopefully. It's the last address for the guy I could find."

"What do we know about him?"

Matt taps at his phone and begins his summation. "Jerry Caldren, thirty-eight, married. Two kids in middle school. Works in the service department at a Chevy dealership. No criminal history. At least, he doesn't have a record."

We both know the lack of a rap sheet doesn't mean he's innocent. Some folks are just plain good at being criminals and don't get caught.

"Anything else?"

"His wife is a cleaning lady. Works for a service in D.C. Before you ask, I couldn't find anything on her working for the Havers when their son was kidnapped."

I nod. If Matt can't find it, I'm prone to believe it doesn't exist. Yes, he's that good. "All right then." I boost myself from the vintage Mustang. "Let's see if Jerry is home."

We climb the steps and my focus once again goes to the imperfect. To the chipping paint along the porch rails and window shutters. I try not to judge, but the house has a worn, tired feel that makes the artist in me groan. With some love, the tiny home would be a historical marvel.

Matt knocks on the rickety screen and steps back. It's nearly five o'clock and I'm hoping Jerry might be home by now.

The interior door swings open and a tall brunette stands there, her gaze flicking between Matt and I. "Can I help you?"

Matt gives her a smile that's neither too bright or phony. Kind, but not memorable. That's what he's shooting for here. Anything more, according to our crack investigator, is overkill.

"Hi." He holds up his business card. "I'm Matt Stephens from the Schock Agency. Is Jerry home?"

Through the screen, she reads the card, gives the extremely studly Matt a once-over, then eyes me. "I'm Meg Schock. Matt and I work together."

After a few seconds, she nods as if I've passed muster. "Hold on."

She closes the door, but we'd have to be deaf not to hear her yelling for Jerry. A minute later, a tall man with dark hair and a long, narrow face is in front of us, stepping onto the porch.

"Hey. What's up?"

I focus on him, looking for any resemblance to Ethan. His eyes are dark and heavy-lidded. His hair is a cross between milk and dark chocolate and for the life of me, I can't see even a hint.

Matt holds his hand out. "Matt Stephens. I'm a PI. This is Meg Schock."

The two men exchange a handshake before Jerry then turns and offers the same to me. He keeps the contact brief and looks at Matt again. "What's this about?"

"We're working a kidnapping case from fifteen years ago."

Jerry lets out a long whistle. "Wow. What's this got to do with me?"

"We got a hit in a DNA database. You're a match to one of the family members involved."

Jerry's head lops forward. "Me? *A kidnapping?*"

"Don't panic." I hold up a hand. "You came up as a cousin to the boy who was kidnapped. We're starting from the beginning."

"Wait. Is he still missing?"

"It's complicated," Matt says. "A boy was recovered eight years ago. DNA analysis confirms he's not who we thought he was. Basically, the wrong child was returned. Now we're trying to find his biological family, as well as locate the missing boy."

Jerry gives his head a hard shake. I don't blame him. "So, like, a switched at birth thing?"

"Not quite," I say. "But the boy was an infant."

"Holy crap."

He could say that again.

Jerry blinks at me, then again. "And I'm a match? Like, he's my kid? No way."

Poor guy. He's starting to freak out and we need him focused. "Mr. Caldren, we didn't say that. He's coming up as a familial match."

"Lady, what the hell does that mean? Do I need a lawyer or something?"

Whoopsie. That's one word we don't necessarily want to hear.

I peer at Matt hoping he'll do something, maybe exchange some kind of male mental telepathy that'll help calm Jerry.

Matt holds his hands palm down. "Relax. You came up as a cousin. We found your profile in the GenCo database."

Jerry tips his head back and lets out a long breath. "Oh. That thing. Yeah. My wife gave me one of those DNA kits as a gift. I tried it. I knew every one of my matches though."

"That's because we just loaded our client's info. He wasn't in there until this week. Now you're coming up as a paternal match. Do any of your cousins on your father's side have sons around fifteen?"

"I have a bunch on his side. There's gotta be forty of them."

Forty.

Terrific.

I roll one hand. "Can you narrow it down for us. Any with teenagers?"

He tips his head one way then the other. "Sure. I've lost touch with half though."

"Can you give us a list?"

His head lops forward again. "Of family members? Are you kidding?"

Dude, I wish I was. "I know this sounds crazy. But anything you can tell us would help. We have a young man who's just found out the people he calls mom and dad are not his biological parents."

"Daddy!"

Jerry looks over my shoulder, peering out to the street. Matt and I turn. There's a young girl with curly dark hair riding her bike along the sidewalk, waving one hand frantically.

"Hi, baby." Jerry hollers. "Both hands!"

Nodding, she grips the handlebars then rides down the alley separating Jerry's house from the neighbor's.

I smile. "Your daughter?"

"Yeah. She's ten. Son is twelve."

"That's nice."

He looks me dead in the eye. "And, yeah, I'd go nuts not knowing where my kid is. Come inside. I'll get you those names."

13

Charlie

*J*ackie DelRay is a spitfire and I remember why I liked her when we helped her and her client, Beck Pearson, last year.

They ended up together, and I see his influence in the suit and heels she wears. Before Beck came along, she favored clothes off the rack from one of the discount chains. Now, she wears designer everything, but it hasn't changed her down to earth, kick-ass style.

She has no love for Lily's shenanigans, and she brings up Lily's YouTube video for me to watch while she calls her office. As she paces, handing out orders to her assistant, I take a deep breath and pray Meg and Matt are having luck with Ethan's biological cousin. On screen, Lily looks at the camera with her perfect makeup, hair, and tears in her eyes.

"Many of you are aware of a pair of private investigators trying to tear my family apart."

I suppress my eyeroll, only because I'm too tired to make the effort. Lily goes on to explain the situation with scant details but plenty of drama. When she's done making me and my sister out to be self-important drama queens intent on ruining her beautiful family and making a name for ourselves at her son's expense, she wipes the tears away and vows to protect Ethan at all costs.

She's an expert at playing it up for the camera and she'll get plenty of sympathy from her viewers. Schock Investigations looks bad to the world, especially me since I'm the agent who brought Ethan home in the first place. Her little act makes me appear an unsympathetic narcissist who has a deep need for attention and admiration.

The psychologist in me thinks the pot's calling the kettle black.

I skipped lunch and my stomach growls so loud I put a hand on it. I'm suddenly tired, too. Exhausted, really. It's been days since I slept more than a few hours at a time. For some reason, having Jackie take control allows me to be human again.

"Hold on a minute," she says to her assistant, "I've got another call." She taps her phone and says, "DelRay."

She listens to whoever is on the other end for about thirty seconds before her whole body swivels toward me, eyes locking on mine. I feel the tiny hairs on the back of my neck stand up.

"Is that so?" she asks. "I see. I assume the formal paperwork will be delivered to my client in the morning?" A pause. Her expression gives nothing away. "Thanks for the heads up."

She ends the conversation and says to me, "Lily has filed a civil lawsuit against you."

Before I can respond, she returns to her conversation, and I'm left with my mouth open.

Man up, I tell myself. I expected this, it's no surprise.

I'm left-brain oriented, and I want the details, the facts. I want to see the paperwork *now*.

"Jackie," I attempt to interrupt her. She holds up a finger and keeps talking.

"Jackie!" I can't help it, I need her full attention.

Her head snaps around, her eyes testy, yet when she sees my face, she puts a hand over the speaker. "What is it?"

"Five minutes," I say. "That's all I need."

She nods tightly and tells her assistant she'll call him back in five minutes on the dot.

"What should I do?" I ask before she finishes disconnecting.

"Nothing," she says. "That's what you have me for. We'll review the official complaint when it comes. Until then, sit on your hands and keep your mouth shut. Are we clear?"

I remind myself I'm paying for this directness. "That's not my style."

I have never sat on my hands in my life, much less kept my mouth shut.

She stalks to the desk and plants both hands on it, leaning toward me. "Look, Charlie, I know this is a ball buster for you, but you have to do what I say to the letter. She's coming after you with both barrels, but I'm your armor. I know you want a resolution to this as fast as possible, but it isn't going to happen. The courts don't move that quickly, which you know, stretching lawsuits out for months, even years. You're going to have to slow your roll and let me drive the bus."

"But–"

She cuts me off with a wave of her hand. "You're paying me a ridiculous sum of money to defend you, we knew this was a possibility, and I'm going to do a stellar job, but the only way this partnership will work is if you follow my directions *to the letter*."

Huh. I may have met someone I can't out argue.

Before I have a chance to form a counterargument, Meg and Matt arrive.

"We've got dozens of people to look into." Meg waves a piece of paper in the air and she walks by my office door. "Hey, Jackie. Conference room meeting, now, Charlie."

Matt sticks his head in and says hi to Jackie more formally. "You okay?" he asks me.

Jackie punches speed dial on her phone, calling her assistant back. "Leave the investigating to them." She hitches a thumb at Matt. "From here on out, you don't touch anything involving Ethan, Carl, or Lily."

Another *but* is on the tip of my tongue. I bite it off and stay silent. This seems to make her happy as she gathers her briefcase. "I'll be in touch tomorrow as soon as we have the lawsuit in hand," she says as she brushes past Matt and disappears.

I rise, square my shoulders, and grab my laptop. "Sounds like you had luck with the cousin."

We head to the conference room, him in the lead. "He gave us quite a list of potential relatives."

At least that's something. I take a seat at the table. "Let me see," I say to Meg and she slides the paper to me.

"I need tea." She jumps out of her chair like her ass is on fire and heads for the door. I wish I had her energy right now. "You guys need anything?"

"I'm good," Matt says.

I need something, but it sure isn't tea. Probably a shot of bourbon. "Nothing for me, thanks."

The handwriting on the paper is atrocious, and I have to reread some of the names twice. Like Meg said, there are dozens. I start counting them off as Matt takes a call from Taylor. "Yeah, babe, I'll be home in a little while." There is a pause, and he furtively glances my way. "She's okay. She's tough like you, and she hired Jackie to help."

Meg returns, and Matt ends his call with Taylor. I draw a

couple of lines on the paper. "We have thirty-four people to investigate, so that's eleven a piece, and I'll take the extra one."

Matt looks at me funny. "What are you doing, Charlie?"

I glance up, confused. "Dividing up the work so one of us doesn't get stuck doing all of it." *Duh.* I don't say that last word, but I think he can read my mind from the way he screws up his face.

Matt shakes his head as if I'm a child who just got caught lying. "Jackie told you to stay away from this."

"What Jackie doesn't know won't hurt her. You guys need help with this, and there's nothing else I can work on at the moment. My hands are tied on everything right now, and I need something to do."

Meg sips her tea. "If Charlie doesn't have something to do, she'll go crazy, which in turn, will make us crazy."

Matt rolls his eyes and holds out his hand for the paper. "I'll make copies."

At ten, we call it quits. Even though we have the names, we don't have contact information for all of them, so we start by looking up numbers and noting those. Tomorrow we can start calling people.

There are a couple of reporters hanging around outside when Meg and I leave, but I don't engage, per Jackie's orders. I do take pictures of them and the license plates numbers on their vans and forward them to her. Meg and I say goodnight to Matt and head home.

We pick up food on the way, and I eat half of mine before we pull into the drive of our duplex. There are two suspicious vehicles on the street and I assume they're more journalists.

As I park, a police vehicle, lights flashing, pulls up behind one of them. The officer gets out, and as Meg and I leave my BMW, I hear him tell the person driving to move on and not bother me or my sister again or he'll issue a ticket.

Meg and I exchange a look and she shrugs. Someone is looking out for us. I assume it's Jackie.

"Get some sleep," Meg says. I told her about the lawsuit, and she had some pretty choice words to say about Lily. "We're going on the offensive tomorrow. She won't know what hit her. I need you in top form."

I appreciate her cheerleading and the fierceness that comes with defending me. After Lily went public, my parents called, several friends, and two of my former FBI colleagues, all to offer support.

A small thing, but an important one. I consider myself a lucky woman, even though my world is starting to split apart.

I promise I'll try to sleep, even though we both know it's a lie.

Inside, I reset my security alarm but make my way through the house in the dark. It's quiet, and for the first time today, I let my guard down. In the kitchen, I turn on a light and find a bottle of wine.

As I pour myself a glass of good merlot, I realize there's light coming from my living room. Everything in me goes on alert, and I draw my gun from the holster at my side.

Silent as a cat, gun ready, I slink forward. My heart beats too fast, every muscle in my body tense as a bowstring.

"Don't shoot me, Charlize," a low, sexy voice says from the couch.

I was wrong about Jackie being the one to keep the media off my doorstep. For the second time in as many days, JJ surprises me. "What are you doing here?" I ask.

His face is tired as he turns to look at me. He must've parked down the block and snuck in the back door so the reporters wouldn't see him.

"I came to check on you, but you weren't here, so I let myself in to wait."

A long time ago, in a weak moment, I gave him a key. Somehow, he bypassed my security alarm too.

I put the gun's safety back on, head to the kitchen and pour a second glass. My heart is beating too fast for a different reason now.

Returning, I hand him one and sit across from him. "I'm sorry. I screwed up."

All the reasons and logical excuses I was going to spell out in my apology desert me.

"I know." He sips the wine and rubs his eyes. "What a clusterfuck."

He doesn't know the half of it. "Lily is suing me."

He nods. "I saw the list."

There's not enough wine in the world to make me feel better tonight, but I take a big drink anyway. For a second, all I can think of is the list of cousins we're investigating to see if they match Ethan's genetic makeup. I don't know why he would've seen that. "You did?"

He swirls the wine, but doesn't drink. "She's suing all of us, your name was at the top."

Shit. A totally different list. "Why?" Silly question, but it pops out before I can stop it.

"Who knows? Because you were head of the taskforce that brought Ethan back?" He shrugs. "Because the kid went to you to show you the results instead of her?"

"I suppose. Feels more personal."

"Suing the FBI and U.S. attorney's office sounds dramatic, but she knows she needs a face to put on this disaster, and she's chosen yours. She needs someone her fans and trolls can attack."

Standing, he shrugs off his jacket, rolls the sleeves of his dress shirt up to his elbows, and plops back down on the sofa, kicking his feet up on my coffee table. He looks so at home here, and I'm more than relieved he seems to have forgiven me.

"I feel like I'm in some weird stasis. I can't go back in time and fix the problem, and I can't seem to find a solution now either. My lawyer told me to keep my hands off the investigation into Ethan's real parents, but most of our other clients fired us after today's media blitz. Can't say I blame them, but I feel..."

"Helpless?"

The wine is an expensive one that I usually enjoy, but I find I can't tonight. It tastes flat. "God, I hate that word."

We sit in silence for long minutes, and I can't help but sneak a look at him. He sees the world much like I do, and our methods for dealing with crime complement each other.

He feels my gaze and lifts his so our eyes meet. "We're signing the papers in two days," he says softly.

My pulse skips a beat. He can't mean... "The divorce papers?"

It's too much to hope for and he hears the excited desperation in my voice. One corner of his mouth kicks up. "I should be a free man by Friday night. Thought maybe we could have a date."

Even with everything else going on, I hop up, throw my hands in the air, splashing wine on myself, and shout, "Hallelujah!"

His grin turns into a full-on smile and he stands, grabs me around the waist, and kisses me.

Reality catches up a few seconds later and I break away gently. "You don't want to date me. Not right now. We can't, in fact, go public about our relationship at all. If anyone gets a whiff of this"—I waggle a finger between us—"and leaks it to the press while this disaster with the Havers is going on, we'll lose whatever shred of credibility we still have in our respective jobs."

He sighs, laying his forehead against mine. He wants to argue, but he knows I'm right.

To my disappointment, he kisses me gently, picks up his jacket, and slips out the back door without another word.

14

Meg

I'm sitting in our conference room, ignoring Fred, the reconstruction I'm behind on, when a knock sounds. I glance up from the files scattered in front of me. Matt is in the doorway looking fresh as a spring morning in dress slacks and a dress shirt with creases so sharp they could slice cement. Then there's me in my Bob Seger concert T-shirt and clay-stained jeans.

I stare at him for a second, bringing my bleary eyes into focus. I've been sitting here since seven this morning, so distracted by the list of family members given to us by Ethan's cousin that I didn't even hear the door chime announce his arrival.

He holds up a manila envelope. "I think I've got something."

This perks me up. I feel like I'm failing miserably with my study of potential suspects so this announcement sends a little tingle down my arms. "What is it?"

I work at keeping my voice even, at not letting hope take me to a place I have no right going. Not this early in the investigation. Charlie constantly warns me against getting emotional and for once, I'm trying damned hard to stay level.

"Ramona Caldren," he says. "She's Jerry's cousin. Their fathers are brothers."

"Okay. What about her?"

"After we left here last night, I made some calls."

I always love when Matt does that. Most of the time, when he's not forthcoming about who they were to, it means he's called in favors that may or may not be legal.

At this point, I don't really care how far outside the lines he plays.

I wave him into the room. "Tell me."

"I was trying to shortcut going through the list. It could take us weeks to find all of them."

"Believe me. I know." I gesture to the files. "I've been at it for hours, figuring out who lives where so we can maximize our time."

"Yeah. Forget that. I have a friend at the Virginia Department of Education."

Oh, this should be good. What they can do for us, I haven't a clue, but I'm a sculptor. What do I know? "And?"

"And, I got to thinking. We're looking for a fifteen-year-old kid. One who, hopefully, is in school somewhere. So I call my friend at VDOE and ask what the chances are he could tell me if any of the folks on our list have a son that meets our criteria."

Matt Stephens. How I love him. "Isn't that illegal?"

He tilts his head and gives me a blank stare. The one that tells me I shouldn't ask too many questions. "Never mind. Did you get a match? Please tell me you did."

"Pack your shit and we'll go see Ramona, who happens to have a fifteen-year-old son with light brown hair—according to his student ID."

He got a photo! "You got a *photo*?"

"Sure did."

"Does he—"

"Look like Carl?" Matt shrugs. "Hard to tell. Maybe. The hair is too light."

"Let me see."

The artist in me can't resist an opportunity to study the angles of the face, the shape of the eyes and nose. Anything, outside of Ethan, that might connect Carl's missing biological son and the Caldrens'.

He holds up the envelope. "It's in here. You can look at it in the car. Let's go."

I leave the folders on the table, knowing Charlie will lose it when she sees the disarray. Too bad. I hop out of my seat, ducking into my office to grab a jacket and my messenger bag. Fred sits on his stand, patiently waiting for me to apply clay strips along his mandible.

"I'll be back soon," I tell him.

Until then, he'll have to wait. At this moment, he is simply a skull with eyeballs secured by stems of clay and I feel the punch of guilt for ignoring him. "I'm sorry, Fred."

This is what my life has come to. Chatting with skulls.

I leave Fred behind and head to the back door. "Haley," I holler over my shoulder. "I'm going with Matt. Call my cell if you need me."

"Okay!" She shouts back.

I hustle out and find Matt already in his car, the purr of the vintage Mustang's engine idling. I climb in the passenger side, buckle up and take the envelope from him. A sheaf of papers inside contains Matt's handwritten notes on Ramona Caldren, a probate attorney at a D.C. law firm.

"No way," I mutter.

"The attorney thing?"

"Yes. I mean, what if Carl and Lily's son is—"

I stop talking. All along I've imagined the kidnappers living in a rotting, nearly condemned

home. The realization strikes that anyone, rich or poor, sane or not, could be a criminal.

"I know, Meg. We can't get ahead of ourselves. There are millions of boys his age in Virginia. Let's just check it out."

More curious than ever if a probate attorney has been raising a kidnapped boy, I shuffle through the stack in search of the photo Matt obtained. Four pages deep, I find what looks like a screenshot from a school database. Ryan Caldren.

Ryan.

Nice name.

Ryan's photo sits at the very top. It's a black and white copy so I can't tell the exact color of the hair though Matt's notes say it's light brown. That's okay. For now, I'm interested in his bone structure.

Matt heads for the expressway while I form a mental picture of Carl and Lily. Hmmm. Now I know why Matt was non-committal. Ryan Caldren, even to my artist's eye, is a completely average teenager. Acne and all. Do I see Carl and Lily in him? Possibly. His jaw, like Carl's, is square and his smile dips—sort of—on one side. Lily flaunted a similar one while building a television career.

But that's all I see. Is it enough?

Who knows?

It could be a bad picture. Or not.

"What do you think?" Matt's voice is casual, but I suspect that's an act.

He loves the hunt and he's hoping as much as I am this is a solid lead.

Still, I can't give him what he wants. "I'm not sure." I shove the papers back in the envelope. "I'd have to see him in person. The photo isn't giving me anything."

Outside my window, trees blur my vision as we speed by.

The full weight of this thing hits me like a branch from one of those sturdy oaks.

In the next hour, we might be shattering the life of Ramona and Ryan Caldren.

I shake my head and let out a sigh. "Lord, what a mess."

"Yep."

We spend the next twenty minutes in silence until Matt turns onto a tree-lined street with elegant brick brownstones and neatly manicured patches of lawn. It screams upscale in a completely understated way and I kinda love it. I could see Charlie living in one of these homes. Me? Not so much. I'm more the simple cottage type.

"Nice," Matt says as we cruise the block looking for number ten-forty-one. Cars dot both sides but given the time, most residents are likely at work leaving plenty of on-street parking.

"It is."

"Kid is lucky to grow up here."

Again, the car goes silent and I wonder if we should do this. Knock on this woman's door and potentially turn her life into a chaotic whirl.

"Then again," Matt adds, "you never know. Nice houses don't mean ideal childhoods."

As a former cop, he'd know.

We park and walk to the oversized front door that must be a find from an antique store. Late eighteen hundreds is my guess.

Matt foregoes the doorbell and knocks. The heavy wood absorbs the pounding, confirming my suspicion of old wood. Doors like this simply aren't made anymore. Someone took great care in finding it.

We wait. And wait. And wait.

"If she's an attorney," I offer, "she's probably at work. Do we have her office address?"

"Yeah. I called there on my way to see you. She's not in today. Figured we'd give here a go."

The door flies open and a woman in her late thirties stands there, headphones around her neck and sweat dripping down her face. She's wearing tights and a tank top and it doesn't take a rocket scientist to realize she must've been working out. Her body is lean and toned, not a soft spot on her and I'm reminded of the treadmill I hang my sweatshirts on.

"Hi," she says, smiling at Matt the hunk and then me.

"Hi. Ramona Caldren?"

"Yes."

Since Ramona clearly likes the looks of Matt, I let him take the lead. We've fallen into a routine on these visits. He does the introductions and acts all Mr. Nice, then I get impatient and move things along. I'd be a terrible investigator. I can sit in front of a sculpture for hours, but don't ask me to play cat and mouse during interviews.

Matt holds out a business card. "I'm Matt Stephens from the Schock agency. This is my associate, Meg Schock."

She takes the card, stares at it for a second and rolls her bottom lip out. "Private investigators?"

"Yes, ma'am."

"All right. I'll bite. What can I do for you?"

How the hell do you tell a woman her son might not be hers? I peer at Matt who refuses to look at me.

"Mrs. Caldren, we're looking into a missing persons case. Our client's son was kidnapped fifteen years ago."

Matt pauses, but I don't dare take my eyes from Ramona. I watch her take in this news, see if there's even a small reaction.

Nothing. Complete deadpan.

Finally, she rolls her hand. "And? What does this have to do with me?"

Clueless.

Or a very good liar. She is a lawyer after all.

Matt leans against the door frame, all Mister Casual. "Our

client's DNA came up as a match with your family. A paternal cousin."

She stares at him for a good three seconds then jerks her head back. At least we're finally getting a reaction out of her.

"Are you saying I have a *cousin* who's missing? Forgive me, but I think we'd know if one of our family members was kidnapped."

Matt gives me a little side eye. A definite indication he wants me to jump in here. Okay. I can do that, but he'd better be prepared for me to screw up. Or, at the very least, say something I shouldn't.

"Mrs. Caldren," I say, "Matt hasn't given you the whole story. Our client's son was kidnapped and found seven years later. He's been living with who we thought were his biological parents ever since. He's now fifteen and through DNA analysis, the family discovered the boy is not their son after all."

Ramona's mouth drops open. "Oh my God. They've been raising the wrong child? That's *horrible*."

"Yes, ma'am. Which is why we're looking into the boy's genetic profile. To see if anyone knows anything."

We spend a few seconds eyeing each other before she steps back, widening the door. "Come in. I'm not sure there's anything I can tell you, but I'm happy to try."

Matt waves me inside to the narrow foyer. Just ahead of me is a large elegant staircase with polished wood that gleams under a crystal chandelier.

Lord, what are we doing? About to ask this woman if her son is the real Ethan Havers? We may be reaching here, but crazier things have happened.

Ramona leads us through a set of oversized sliding doors separating the hallway from a large living room. Like the rest of the house, the walls are a pale gray. Ramona points to the sitting area where four deep blue chairs are situated in front of the fireplace.

We take the two on the left and Ramona sits across from us. On the mantle are an array of photos. Ramona and a young boy. A man with the same boy. Ramona and the man. None of the three of them together, but someone, I assume, had to take the picture.

"My son," she says when she sees my attention has wandered. "And husband."

I look over at her and nod. "Nice family."

"Thank you. They're my world. Now, about your client. Can you tell me anything about him?"

Her gaze pops between Matt and I until I hold my hand to Matt. He's the expert here so I'll let him answer the hard questions.

He nods and faces Mrs. Caldren. "Nothing more than what we've already said. Privacy reasons."

Matt and I stay silent while Ramona peers at the photos of her son. "Poor kid. He's the same age as my son."

Yep. Sure is.

She snaps back to us. "Wait. Do you... Are you here because you think...?" She stops. "Oh, my God."

"We don't think anything, ma'am."

"Oh, bull*shit*. I'm tight with most of my cousins. If you'd been to see a few already, I'd have heard about it. You saw I have a son the same age as your client and you came to me first. You *cannot* think your client is mine. That, what? We switched them? Why would I do that?"

Matt holds up his hands. "Whoa, we didn't say that. We're investigating any leads. And, sure, the fact that your son is the same age is an interesting starting place. That's all we're doing, gathering information."

"Well, gather all you like. My son is *my* child. I have no doubt. You want a DNA test, I'll give you one. We have nothing to hide."

I lean forward and rest my elbows on my knees. "Thank

you. I don't know that it's necessary, but if it comes to that, we'd appreciate it."

Ramona studies me for a second. "I feel bad for your client, but you're way off here. I can prove he's my son right now."

Matt and I exchange a what-the-fudge? look as she rises and walks to a drum table near the front window. She opens the drawer, shuffles through the contents and extracts a photo.

Returning to us, she holds out the photo and Matt latches on to it as I lean over to peek. The photo is of a little boy, maybe three or four years old. He has light brown hair and a wide smile with baby teeth that have yet to fall out. On his left cheek is a large mole.

One that would be impossible to miss.

"That's my son," Ramona says. "He was three." She lifts one of the framed photos from the mantle. "This is him last summer. See the mole? It's in all his baby pictures. It was removed when he was nine." She points to the framed picture, an extreme close-up that looks like it might be a school photo. "You can see the scar in this picture. Did your client have a mole?"

Matt's face remains neutral. His cop face, Charlie calls it.

"No, ma'am," he says. "No mole."

Ramona Caldren, it seems, is a dead end.

15

Charlie

*W*hen Meg calls to tell me about Ryan Caldren, to cross him off the list, I feel inordinately depressed.

Jackie told me not to go near the office today, so when I called and Haley told me Meg and Matt had taken off together, I felt a spurt of hope. I knew they had a lead, so even though Meg didn't let me know what or who it was, I could barely sit still.

"You still there, Charlie?" she asks.

I force my voice not to betray me. "Yeah. It was a good lead. Thanks for trying."

"Have you come across anything you want us to follow-up on while we're out? Can we bring you some lunch?"

She knows me so well, knows I'm wearing a hole in the floor of my living room. She wants to take care of me, but really, what can she do? "I'm good. Just working on my part."

My phone buzzes with an incoming call, but I ignore it. My personal number got leaked to the world, and the media is intent on getting a statement.

Jackie and I reviewed the lawsuit Lily is bringing against me, and I honestly have no statement. She assures me it'll get thrown out before she's done with it, and Lily will have to be content to go after the others on her list. I feel numb at this point.

I texted JJ her number, recommending he hire Jackie for the battle ahead. He hasn't responded, but I can hear him telling me we shouldn't share the same attorney. Not only is the media hounding me, I've already received a few threats from the public. Apparently, as Lily must have surmised, this story has hit a sore spot with a lot of people. I'm being called a home-wrecker, a joke of an agent, and worse.

The FBI is taking a pounding, too, so I draw some comfort from that. Unfortunately, any of the cases I worked during my tenure with them are now being called into question. Before the week is over, I wouldn't be surprised if each one has to be reopened.

Along with that, every trial I testified in, for or against the defendant, could be thrown out due to misconduct and need to be retried.

I'm living my worst nightmare.

"Charlie?" Meg's voice brings me back to our conversation.

"Sorry, mind travel. What did you say?"

"Dad left me a message a little while ago. He and mom are bringing food tonight for the four of us. We can do it at my place, if you're not up to hosting."

I love her and my parents for taking care of the routine things like eating. I know it's more than that, sharing dinner. They're bringing me support.

My first instinct is to say I'm fine and tell her meeting here is too. Instead, I admit I'd rather not try to make my place presentable, because right now it's in as much chaos as my brain. "I could use a chance to get out of these walls for a couple hours."

My phone buzzes again, and this time I look to see if I recognize the number. I think it might be JJ, or Jackie, but it's neither. "Hold on, Meg." My pulse picks up as I recognize the number. "Ethan's calling."

"Don't hang up. I want to know what he says."

I put her on hold and answer. "Ethan? Is everything okay?"

He should be at school, but knowing him, he's faking being sick again. Before he speaks, however, I hear the sound of kids talking in the background, the clink of silverware and the clatter of trays. "I think I found him, Charlie."

"Who?"

"I'm sorry about what my mom did, but I think she may have helped us. This kid, he saw the story, and tracked me down. He messaged me through iWhisper. He wants to chat after school today. He thinks he's me."

The clever app is designed to look like a music manager, but kids use it for chatting, sharing photos and videos, and free texting and calls they don't want parents knowing about. I only know thanks to Matt, who keeps Meg and I up to date on these things. "You mean, he thinks he's the real Ethan?"

"Yeah."

This could be a dead end, a kid who's mistaken, or trying to pull fast one. "What's his name?"

"He goes by Arrow."

I sigh. Smart kid, only using a screen name. At least, I assume it's a fake. "What time are you chatting?"

"Four. He thinks his mom's...weird. Like, he's always felt she wasn't really his."

"He's not adopted?"

A clang in the distance as if someone dropped a tray. "I don't think so."

"Can you copy and forward the message to me?"

"They disappear two minutes after you read them." He says this as if I'm a child he has to explain things to. "But I copied part of our chat. I'll text it to you."

Thank goodness Ethan is also a smart kid. "Is your mother expecting you home right after school?"

"Yeah, but she won't be there. She's doing an interview about you with some journalist."

Great. But this helps. "Can you meet me at my office? I'll have Matt—a cool guy who works for me—pick you up, if you're okay with that."

"My dad said we should do whatever we need to in order to straighten this out, so sure. But there are tons of reporters milling around here, trying to get a picture of me. Can he get me at the Gas You Up two blocks over? I can get there without them following me."

It's become a cloak and dagger operation. I could get burned for this, but how much worse can my situation get? "What time? Meg will be with him. He drives a blue vintage Mustang. You know what that is, right?"

"Duh, of course. I'll be at the Gas around three-ten. See you after school!"

He hangs up and a few seconds later, my cell dings with his text. *Arrow232: I don't know who you are, but I may be Ethan Havers. The real one. My mom isn't really my mom, I'm sure of it. Can we chat @4?*

I take a deep breath and let it out slowly, then click back to Meg. "On second thought, I have a new lead for you."

"Tell me," she demands.

"Pick up Ethan at the convenience store two blocks from his school at three-ten."

"Hot damn," she says. "Why?"

"The real Ethan Havers may have found us."

16

Meg

We scoop Ethan up at the gas station at precisely three-ten—this kid is good—and head to the office. In the backseat of Matt's car, Ethan's energy is snapping like a downed live wire.

"This could be it," he says.

Determined to keep him from getting his hopes too high, I peer over my left shoulder. "*Could.* We're not sure yet though so try and stay neutral. Okay? I know it has to be hard."

Matt stops at a light and eyes Ethan in the rearview. "She's right. We see stuff like this a lot. After your mom's press conference, all kinds of crackpots are coming out of their holes. Bastards."

Ethan's adorable face pops between the bucket seats and he swings his head from me to Matt and back. "I know, but this could be *it.*"

When I don't respond, he sits back with a pinched mouth

that gives him a...well...pissy expression. I feel for him, but we can't allow a fifteen-year-old to count on things he shouldn't be. He's already had one trauma this week finding out Carl and Lily aren't his parents.

Plus, Taylor called Matt thirty minutes ago, telling him they'd received five hundred tips on the Havers' case. It appeared everyone wanted to cash in on their fame. Now we have a full-blown shitshow with Ethan taking center stage.

Anger whirls into a ball between my shoulder blades. What the hell was Lily thinking going public like that? Given her husband's celebrity status, not to mention her own platform, she should've known better. Now every news outlet wants a piece of Ethan. All because his mother threw him to the wolves.

At some point, after we sort this mess out, I may have to give her a piece of my mind.

"She didn't mean it."

This from our mutinous friend.

I turn to Ethan who stares at me with wide, chocolate brown eyes heavy with sadness. Cripes, the mood swings of teenagers are maddening.

Still, I want to wrap him in a hug. His world, quite literally, has been ripped away from him.

"Excuse me?"

"My mom. Lily. She didn't mean to create problems for me. She just...you know...doesn't know what to do."

Lacking any sort of a decent answer, I turn forward again. Arguing with a teenager never amounts to anything. Plus, given the situation, I'm not about to tell Ethan his mother is a self-centered witch.

The remainder of the ride continues in awkward silence and I'm grateful when Matt pulls into his usual spot in our back parking lot.

My mood perks up when I spot an ancient Toyota in remarkably good shape beside my van.

I slide out and hold the seat for Ethan while keeping an eye on Jerome in the driver's side of his car. What he's doing here, I have no idea. It's not that he hasn't visited before. He just usually calls or texts first. He's broken routine.

Once Ethan is out, I tell them to head inside and I'll meet them.

Matt eyeballs me, then the Toyota. "Jerome?"

"Yes. I don't want to bring him inside with Ethan here."

"Don't stay out here long. Reporters are like cockroaches."

"I'll be fine. Go on."

Jerome's door pops open and he eases his long legs out with that laid-back quality I've grown to love. He's wearing his typical garb of torn jeans and a graphic T-shirt with psychedelic swirls and a peace sign. His hair falls around his face in a messy array of waves and he shoves his hand through it as he walks toward me.

I love that hair. On rainy days it curls at the ends giving him a shaggy look that makes my heart thump.

What am I doing?

I really have no idea. I want him. I don't want him. The truth is, I'm chicken.

We both know it.

I smile as I approach and open my arms, offering a hug that is not customary for us, but isn't exactly foreign either. We've done it before. Many times. It usually ends with one of us backing away and staring at the ceiling. Hello, awkward.

Today, I hang on. The last few weeks have done me in. First, the crazed serial killer and now a lost teenager. How much emotion is one empath supposed to take?

Jerome's arms tighten around me and I squeeze my eyes shut. My body folds into his much taller one as I take every ounce of affection he's willing to give. I've never been one to need a man, but it'd be nice to have an outlet at times. Someplace other than a river to seek refuge.

Now, standing in the parking lot, wrapped in Jerome's arms, I understand how Charlie feels about JJ.

And that scares the crap out of me.

"Hi," he finally whispers.

His breath is warm on my ear, sending a little zing right to my toes.

"Hi."

I ease away and stare into the hazel eyes I've painted hundreds of times. "What are you doing here?"

"Came to see you."

"Usually you call."

He shrugs. "I know. Uh, we have an audience."

I turn and spot Matt standing in the doorway, his protective gaze on Jerome. They've met before, but I think Matt suspects Jerome is my supplier and as a former cop, I'm not sure he knows how to deal with that.

"Inside," I tell him for the third time.

I angle back to Jerome, but he's still watching where Ethan and Matt entered.

"That was him," he says. "The sketch you had me do. Is that the kid you hoped it looked like?"

"Yep."

After Lily's press conference, Ethan's face has been plastered all over the media so there's no sense denying anything.

"I came close."

"Really close. It's baffling."

"Why?"

"Because he's not the real Ethan. His DNA doesn't match his parents."

"Oh, man. Poor kid."

"Yeah."

"Wait. The press conference. The woman married to the anchorman. *That's* your case?"

If Charlie were here, she'd be stroking out. I have two choices. I can lie or fall back on client confidentiality.

Lying isn't my style.

I guess I'll pick door number two. "Jerome, I can't—"

"You can't talk about it."

He's given me the out and yet, I don't want it. Right or wrong, I want the connection that comes with sharing things. And I want it with him.

"I shouldn't talk about it, but you helped us, and I trust you. Yes, that's him. Ethan Havers."

A cocky grin lifts one side of his mouth. "You do, huh?"

After all this time it shouldn't be a shock, but I know this man and he's fishing for a compliment so I give it to him. "Yes."

"Good. That's part of why I'm here."

All righty then. Where exactly is this going? "Do tell, Jerome."

"Our conversation the other day. When you said you loved me."

Oh.

That.

Lord, I hope that little admission doesn't bite me on the rear. The last thing I need is to scare my most cherished friend off.

"Yes?"

"What if I don't want to be stuck anymore?"

17

Charlie

"Where's Meg?" I ask Matt when he and Ethan enter my office.

"Out talking to *Jerome*." It's amazing the way he can put so much emphasis in a word. He says the man's name like he's the bane of Matt's existence. "Want me to get her?"

Jerome. I sigh. "No, let her have her fun. Hi, Ethan."

"I'm changing my name," he announces as he plops into the chair across from me. "What do you think of Carter?"

"Sounds like a president," I say. "Seems like a nice guy, I guess."

He screws up his face. "Austin?"

Matt chirps up. "The capital of Texas?"

Ethan glances between us, sees Matt grinning, and throws his hands in the air. "I'm serious. I can't go around being Ethan anymore."

At least he's not a bucket of emotions, or yelling at me, like everyone else. Out of all the people involved, Ethan should be the most upset, and yet he's acting the most mature. This is what I love about kids. "Who's your favorite sports star?"

"Bryce Harper."

I don't follow sports so the name means nothing to me. "That sounds like a good name."

Ethan seems to consider it and Matt gives me a covert thumbs-up for humoring the kid. He rubs his hands together and leans forward. "It's almost four o'clock."

Ethan comes out of the chair and around to my side of the desk, setting his phone in front of me. He taps the iWhisper icon and opens a chat window.

"I want all this documented before it disappears," I tell him. This could be another dead end, but the fact he contacted Ethan, rather than his parents calling the Havers or the FBI has my hopes up.

Of course, it could be some lunatic pretending to be a teenager, but it's the strongest lead I have since I've been shut out of the case. "We need proof he's legitimate, so I'll give you some instructions as we go along, got it?"

Matt relaxes into the other chair. "Charlie knows what she's doing, Ethan."

"Dude," Ethan says with exasperation, "like, I get it. Not going to screw it up, okay?"

Four o'clock comes and goes with no Arrow232 joining Ethan's chat. Every minute or so, Ethan checks another messaging app, his Snapchat feed, and Twitter. This kid has more social media connections than I do with law-enforcement.

A *ding* sounds and he flips back to the iWhisper app. "It's him."

Matt comes around to look over my shoulder.

Arrow232: *yo, sorry I'm late. Mom problems.*

"Ask about her," I instruct.

Ethan: *no prob. I totally get that. Mine's extra right now.*

"Extra what?" I ask, keeping my voice low even though that's silly—Arrow can't hear us.

"You know, like overly dramatic."

Teenager slang—I'm rusty on it, especially in the cyberspace world.

Arrow232: *she's always weird, but...*

Ethan: *but what?*

Arrow232: *she's riled up since she heard about you. Paranoia, bro. Like she checks our locks six times a night, won't let me go anywhere right now. I tried to find my birth certificate, on the down low. IDK. It's not in any of my baby stuff. I don't look like her AT ALL. There's no pictures of her, you know, pregnant with me, or anything.*

Nothing too damning there. "Ask about his father."

Ethan does and the reply ups my hope.

Arrow232: *I don't know who he is. She'd never tell me. There are no records I can find. No pictures, no nothing.*

"How did she enroll him in school without a birth certificate?" Matt asks.

"She may have one in a safe deposit box," I say to Matt, then to Ethan, "Ask why he thinks he's you, specifically."

Ethan: *so you think you could be me, bro? Why?*

Arrow232: *I look like that sketch when you were younger. Seriously, we could be brothers. Saw it on the news, looked it up online to see it up close. My school picture at that age looks exactly like you.*

Mom is upset after seeing the news about Ethan—could be she's imagining herself in Lily's shoes. Dad is out of the picture —nothing terribly unusual about that. Arrow232 thinks he looks exactly like Ethan. Might help if we could verify that before we go farther.

"We need a picture," I tell Ethan. "Then and now, if possible."

Ethan relays the message as a question. The boy comes

back with an affirmative—*give me a sec.*

In the intervening moments, my pulse trips over itself. Dead end or the break we've been waiting for?

Matt and I exchange a look. He's thinking the same, and wondering how much trouble he'll be in with Taylor if this somehow gives us the correct Ethan.

Any leads should go through the FBI, we both know that, but Matt and I also believe it's better to beg forgiveness than ask for permission.

I have to admit my ego has a lot riding on this. If Arrow232, by some miracle, turns out to be our kid, and I'm the one who reunites him with Carl and Lily, it'll take a little of the tarnish off my reputation.

More than that, it'll help me sleep better. My conscience is a tough taskmaster, and I'll never fully get over this mistake, but righting it will go a long way in me hating myself less.

Ethan quickly checks his other social media accounts while we wait. I wonder if this impatience is normal teenager behavior, or he's as nervous as I am and trying not to show it.

Bottom line, he has more riding on this than I do. Some deeply buried motherly instinct makes me want to hug him and tell him everything will work out.

I drop my fingers on the desktop, consider getting up and grabbing a cup of coffee. The watched pot never boils, my mother always says, and that's how I feel at this moment. Maybe if I get up and go do something, anything, he'll get those damn pictures to us faster.

I stand, and Matt grins, once more keying into my emotions. He knows I hate waiting, especially for something as potentially important as this.

Before I can step away, Meg appears in the door. I sense someone—Jerome—behind her, but he stays out of view. "Sorry," she says. "I got distracted. How's it going?"

"No proof yet. We're waiting on pictures. This kid thinks he looks exactly like the sketch you did when Ethan was seven."

"Bryce," the kid corrects me.

I ignore him. "Claims he's a dead ringer for our Ethan." I pat him on the shoulder. "We don't even know his real name yet, but we might as well see him first."

"I'm changing my name to Bryce," Ethan tells her.

"Well, okay then. I'm still calling you Ethan until that's official." She steps into the room, and hitches a thumb over her shoulder. "By the way, I found this guy in the parking lot."

Expecting to see Jerome, I'm surprised when JJ steps in. He's not in a suit, but casual slacks and a polo. I rarely see him like this and that adds to my surprise.

I hold up my hands in mock surrender, ready to be chewed out about what I'm doing. "I swear, we're going to call Taylor as soon as we verify this is a legitimate lead."

He glances between me and Ethan, nodding at the kid who has stopped his social media scan. "I'm not here to give you grief about whatever it is you're doing. In fact, if you need help, I'm free."

The way he says it sends warning bells clanging in my head. "What happened?"

He sighs and sinks his hands into his pockets. "I'm on suspension."

We all look at him in shock. "You can't be serious," I say.

Before he can respond, Ethan's phone dings, and my pulse goes crazy again. He opens the chat room window.

"Holy crap," he says.

I'm glancing over his shoulder, and that's my initial reaction too.

"Let me see," Meg says.

First, Ethan pulls up a photo of the sketch Meg did eight years ago side-by-side with a class picture.

The young boy in the school photo does indeed favor Carl and looks enough like Ethan to be his brother.

Ethan uses his finger to scroll up to the next—another side-by-side shot. A current selfie of the boy we're chatting with holding up Ethan's picture from the news.

Ethan stares like he's seeing his doppelgänger, and perhaps he is.

I do a mental fist pump. "Get his name as well as his mother's," I tell Ethan, "but don't make any promises. We need to research this thoroughly before we get ahead of ourselves and create an even worse situation."

He starts typing.

To Matt, I say, "Notify Taylor you have a potential lead,"—*keep my name out of it*— "but you want to keep it quiet for now. We don't want to upset another family until we have solid evidence to go on."

Plus, if this kid's mother is a criminal who participated in the kidnapping, I don't want her alerted to the fact we're on her trail.

But this will keep Matt out of trouble down the road, regardless of what we find. He nods and leaves the room.

"Got it," Ethan says, showing me the phone.

Jon and Anita Baker. No wonder the kid uses an odd Avatar name—Jon is so common.

"Good job." I pat him on the shoulder again and scribble their names on a sticky note. "Tell him you have friends who'll look into it and you'll be in touch within the next twenty-four hours, but ask him to keep silent about it for now."

The last thing I want is to rip someone else's life apart if this doesn't pan out.

And if there is something fishy about his mom, I need to know before she can disappear with Jon in tow.

Ethan nods and I rip the yellow note from the pad and hand it to Meg. JJ reads it over her shoulder.

"Let's get to work," I say. "I want to know everything about Jon and his mother, Anita Baker, and I want to know it now."

18

Meg

It's been an active few minutes. First, Jerome hits me with the idea of wanting to be unstuck, then JJ informs us of his suspension and Ethan—God bless him—has possibly found his brother from another mother.

Every one of my chakras might be blown. Completely busted to smithereens.

I'll deal with that later. Along with Jerome, whose revelation damn near knocked me back a step, before JJ interrupted us. I was never so happy to see the emperor. Does that make me horrible? Probably.

All I know is I wasn't ready to answer Jerome's question. I adore him. More than likely, I could love him. Love-love him. Easily.

But relationships don't always work out and losing him would kill me.

Yes, I'm chicken. Afraid to emotionally move forward with him.

And I sure as hell can't contemplate that when we may possibly find the real Ethan soon.

I slap my hands together. "Okay. What can I do?"

Charlie keeps her gaze glued to the notepad she's furiously scribbling on. "Give me two minutes. Everyone go. JJ, you stay."

I tap Ethan on the shoulder. "Come on, kid. I'll get you a soda. Do your parents know where you are?"

"They think I'm at a student body meeting. If they check my location though, I'm busted."

"Do they normally do that?"

"Only when I don't immediately respond to texts. They're paranoid that way."

Understandable, considering he's a kidnapping survivor.

I step around JJ into the hallway with Matt and Ethan in tow. Matt heads for his office, no doubt to call Taylor and fill her in. And keep himself out of trouble. I feel for him. He's stuck with his future bride on one side and Charlie and I on the other. Rational thought tells me he should align with Taylor, but this situation defies logical thinking. Involving the FBI always brings complications. More eyes on the case may not be a bad thing, but the spin-factor could lead to a total loss of control.

Once they take over, we're out. And they'll make quick work using Charlie as their sacrifice.

A loud bang sounds on the front door. After the run-in with a serial killer, we try to keep them locked, but admittedly, we're all getting used to that and sometimes forget. Habits die hard and this one is no exception. It's also a nasty confrontation with the reality of our world. We are no longer safe in our own office.

Simply devastating.

It sounds again, harder this time and enough to stop me in the center of the hallway. Matt pauses at his door and eyes me.

"Ethan," I point to the breakroom. "Have a seat in there. Check the fridge for snacks and sodas. I'll be there in a sec."

He shrugs and moves off while Matt and I head for the reception area where Haley is already at the door.

"Hang on," Matt says.

The knock comes again. "Charlize Schock! Open up."

Female voice. Who the heck?

Haley steps back, hands up as if the handle has fried her skin. I hustle to the window and peep out the blinds. Standing there are Lily Havers, and another woman—a blonde—with heavy make-up and big hair and...oh, no.

A camera man.

I tip my head back. I'll need to meditate for a week. "Crap."

Matt steps toward me, his big body moving fast as he morphs to beast mode. "What is it?"

I shove my arm out to block him from the window. "It's Lily. With a camera man and, I assume, a reporter."

"Charlize Schock!" The reporter yells. "Open this door. With or without you, we're live in two minutes talking about your incompetence surrounding the Havers case and your affair with JJ Carrington."

My jaw drops.

That witch. Lily knows, *knows*, that JJ was an up-and-coming prosecutor during the original investigation. At the time, they were nothing more than acquaintances. Any hint of impropriety between him and the lead agent on a case could wreck both their careers. This, I will not have.

No, sir.

Charlie and JJ appear in the hallway and I meet my sister's gaze. "Go back in your office. Both of you. I've got this."

The dead last thing we need is this news crew finding him here. I was outside with JJ and didn't see any news vans, so we may have caught a break there.

My sister takes a step closer—damn her—and something

churns inside me. She's so used to taking charge she can't see she's about to run headlong into a disaster.

I jab my finger at her. "Stop. Right there." I stomp toward them as the yelling outside continues. "That's Lily Havers and a camera crew out there. Do you want them seeing the two of you in here? Get back in your office and let me deal with it. Go."

JJ's head snaps back and Charlie props her hands on her hips as she skewers me with a look that's all who-the-hell-do-you-think-you-are.

I'm a baby sister that's had enough. *That's* who I am.

On any other day, I'd find their reactions humorous. After the last several weeks, between the serial killer and now this? I'm done.

I square my shoulders and meet her gaze. "Don't *fuck* with me on this. We have everything to lose here. I'm a partner in this agency. It's not just you on the line. And then there's JJ."

At the mention of him, or possibly my dropping the f-bomb, Charlie's eyebrows hike up. Yes, my sister's reasonable self has returned.

"Charlie." JJ reaches for her, setting his big hand on her arm. "As much as it's killing me, let Meg handle it."

"One minute!" The bitch of a reporter screams.

Charlie stares at the door a few seconds then comes back to me. "Fine. Don't screw it up."

Nothing like a vote of confidence from the mighty Charlie Schock.

I turn away and head to the door, checking behind me before opening it to make sure the happy couple are out of sight.

"Meg," Matt says.

I hold up my hand. I don't need additional chatter. What I need is five damned seconds to settle myself. I do it. Just stand there with my hand in Matt's face while I close my eyes and take a deep breath. Then another. *Breathe.* In and out. *Breathe.*

Mercifully, the reporter has paused her yelling.

Breathe. Three, two, one.

I open my eyes and turn to Matt, meeting his crystal blue gaze. "I've got this."

"I know you do. All I was going to say is I'll come out with you."

Such a good guy. I'm so grateful. "Thank you. You're...amazing."

"Charlize Schock!"

Oh, this bitch. I rip open the door. "Stop that goddamned yelling."

Whoa! Not exactly the calm approach, but whatever.

"Meg," Lily spits out, as if my name is acid on her tongue. "I want to speak to your sister."

Beside me, Matt places his hand on my lower back, offering a warning pat. I can't get sucked into a brawl with Lily. Not on camera.

Right now I need to be Charlie-lite. Confident, poised and assertive.

Charlie-lite.

I step outside crowding Lily and the reporter. They move back. My first victory. *Yay, me.*

Behind me, Matt closes the door, letting Lily and her blonde cohort know this will end on our doorstep.

I face the blonde. "Who are you?"

"I'm Joclyn Blanchard from Crime Weekly."

Crime Weekly? Seriously? After looking like the wounded mother on YouTube, Lily coming to our door with an organization known for sensational—and often-times untrue— reporting won't win her any credibility. Then again, maybe she's not interested in the truth.

Perhaps all Lily wants is attention. Any way she can get it.

This from the wife of a nationally recognized news anchor.

The reporter flaps a hand at the lone cameraman. "Make

sure you're getting this." She shoves a microphone at me. "What do you make of the allegations that Charlize is sleeping with JJ Carrington? That they used the Havers kidnapping to further their careers?"

My poor sister. This is her worst nightmare. Whether we're live or they're simply taping, I need to fix this. I face Lily, the traitorous bitch who's betrayed my sister.

"Lily, you know Charlie worked night and day on Ethan's case. I have no idea what you're doing right now, but you should stop. Before I'm forced to defend my sister from these horrible allegations. Unlike Charlie, I have no problem letting out whatever secrets of yours she uncovered during her investigation. And, just a reminder, I sat in your house the other day and watched you and Carl snipe at each other. America's sweethearts didn't look too sweet to me. If I were you, I'd think long and hard about how comfortable you are with your personal life becoming public fodder."

My slamming pulse warns me that I've taken the mother of all fliers. Outside of what Charlie has told me, I'm clueless as to what's in her case files.

But, we all have secrets.

Lily's eyes flash and a bout of smugness slows my raging heart rate.

"Lily," the reporter says, "what's she talking about?"

"You bitch," Lily hisses at me.

"Me? You put your fifteen-year-old son's case out there for public consumption then come to our door spewing this nonsense and *I'm* the bitch? I think you'd better take a good long look in that mirror you're so fond of. There's a whole lot of ugliness to be seen." Now I face Joclyn. "Get your facts straight before we sue you and your show." I lean in a little, lowering my voice the way folks do when they want to make a point. "I will bury you. Now get off our property. Right now."

19

Charlie

I'm stunned, Ethan watching with me as Meg takes on Lily, the live broadcast on his phone.

The kid is as devastated as I am, which says something about his level of compassion—which the woman who's been his mother all this time doesn't seem to possess.

Meg comes storming into the room. "Before you bawl me out, I had to do something to get her off our butts."

I stand and hug her. "Thank you. You did great."

"I tried to channel you." She smiles.

"You always have my back, and I appreciate it." The words feel insignificant for what she's done. "Thank you," I say again.

JJ rubs a hand over his face, as dumbfounded as I am. I sink low in my chair and drop my head into my hands. "How the hell did she find out about us?"

I seem to have taken the steam out of Meg and she glances between me and JJ. "I didn't confirm anything."

"Doesn't matter," JJ tells her. "The cat's out of the bag. If there's even a hint of impropriety, a whiff that we have a personal relationship, regardless of the fact we didn't during the Havers' investigation, it smacks of personal misconduct and conflict of interest. I'll be lucky if I'm not suspended for six months or longer. I'll probably lose my job."

My god, my god, my god. This thing has spun so out-of-control, I don't know what to do. I feel mentally paralyzed.

I sink lower in my chair, sliding halfway down and blow air out my lips. "And every case we worked together while I was an agent could be thrown out and need to be retried."

Matt hangs in the doorway. "Only if they have proof, Charlie, which I assume they don't, since the two of you would never do anything immoral or unethical like that, right?"

He knows me well.

JJ does too. "A mere allegation of misconduct is not a sufficient basis for prosecutorial recusal," he says, as if convincing himself as much as me, "or in this situation, enough for anyone to reopen cases and start throwing them out."

A mere allegation. Sounds so...quaint.

I never thought I'd be airing my sex life in front of everyone, but what the hell? "There was no *misconduct* while I was with the FBI working cases with you, and there's no evidence to suggest otherwise."

"We'll still come under investigation," JJ says, preparing me for something I'm already dreading, "but only if my supervisor or a judge determines Lily's accusations are serious enough to warrant an official one."

"I think you should sue that bitch," Meg says, and then clears her throat when she remembers *that bitch* has been the woman Ethan believed was his mother for the past eight years. "What she's doing is slander. Call Jackie right now."

"Wait." The kid frowns between me and JJ. "You two hooked up?"

JJ looks like he could bite a bullet in two. He's probably shearing enamel off his teeth.

"I'm sorry," I say. To all of them. I'm not sure I can sink any lower. "I'm so, so sorry."

"Well, I'm sure not going home," Ethan says. "I can't believe she did this to me. I mean, I thought she cared about me, even if I'm *not* her biological son."

"Of course she does," I argue, although I have some doubts. My heart is in my stomach. "Where will you go? You're a minor, and right now, everyone's watching you. There could be dangerous people out there who would do you harm if you're on your own."

"I'll take him with me," Meg volunteers.

"Not without permission from his legal guardian," JJ tells her.

She waves him off and heads for the door. "I'll call Carl."

"No," Ethan says, phone in hand. "I will."

Twenty minutes later, my sister has written permission faxed over from Carl to keep him with her. Ethan, apparently, knows how to play the media card as well as Lily and threatened to contact the ABC affiliate and do a live interview if Carl didn't agree.

Being a smart man, he allowed it, but insisted on getting hourly texts from Ethan to ensure his safety.

Carl even brought him a suitcase of clothes. It doesn't sit well with me. Lily gave the boy up to a feeding frenzy by the media; Carl gave him up, at least temporarily, to my sister, as if he were a family pet. Even if the kid did make threats, I want Carl to fight for him. To protect him and not worry about his own damned image.

I call Jackie and get her assistant. She has other clients to take care of, and even though my world is falling apart, hers goes on. I'm assured she'll call me later, and though I understand, I feel let down.

The call that comes in five minutes later is not from Jackie. "I was sitting here talking to your mother," my dad says, "and I think after your little problem is resolved, we should all go up to the cabin near the lake in North Carolina. You remember the place, Charlize? We went there when you were fifteen."

"Hi, Dad." My father doesn't mention the latest wrinkle, and I could hug him for that. I'm sure he's seen it on the news. "I do remember it, very fondly, in fact. I think it'd be wonderful to go with you guys for a weekend sometime."

I don't really have time to discuss future vacation plans with him, although I sure wish I did, but I sense there's a reason behind this call. It's better than him phoning and saying, "Geez, Charlie, you sure have yourself in a pile of shit."

Which is probably what he's thinking, but he also believes in me, in the idea I can get myself out of this situation.

"You should bring that friend of yours, Carrington, when we go. I want to check him out, make sure he's good enough for my little girl."

And *there* it is. He did see Lily's stunt and knows about us now. "I'll be sure to invite him."

JJ, sitting across from me, looks up from his folded hands and gives me a curious stare. I assure my father I'm doing okay, as is Meg, and yes, we'll be over Sunday for dinner if possible.

When I hang up, I tell JJ, "The Spanish Inquisition is coming in the form of my father."

"Should I be scared?"

"Terrified."

We share a smile, and for just a second, I feel a little better. *Thanks, Dad.*

Lily and her media friend leave, and we disguise Ethan and sneak him out the back and into Meg's van. They plan to get dinner before going to Meg's.

Haley leaves for the day. Matt goes back to contacting Jerry Caldren's cousins. JJ and I dig into Jon and Anita Baker.

We come up with zilch, and eventually Matt calls it a day. JJ and I are left alone, and I wonder if there are reporters outside watching. There's no way I can sneak him out, and knowing him, he wouldn't let me anyway. I'm waiting for the background check to come in on Anita when he offers to order in food.

"I need to get out of here," I tell him. I have the feeling Jackie's not going to call today, and I'm itching to do something besides look at a computer screen. "We can't exactly be seen together in public, but I can pick up Thai on the way home and meet you at my place. Early dinner. Let me leave first, then if there are reporters, they'll follow me, and you can make a clean getaway."

He grins, although it doesn't reach his eyes. "Oh, how the mighty have fallen."

I force myself to say the words I've been stewing over the last few hours. "How is Carlena going to take the news about us?"

Carlena Gage Carrington will pitch a fit, I have no doubt. I wonder if she'll use this as leverage in the divorce. *So close*, I think. We were so damn close to having her out of our lives.

JJ probably worries the same, but he shrugs it off. "She's known there was someone for a while. She was bound to find out it was you by this weekend."

"She's going to rake you over the coals."

He puts both hands on the conference table and pushes to his feet. "She already has."

He says it as if he's thinking *bring it on.*

I stand, looking him directly in the eye. "I'm not worth it. You should cut your losses and run."

He comes around, so he's right in front of me. "You're not getting rid of me that easy."

He kisses me, deeply and passionately, nearly bending me over the table. I'm not sure where it would've led, but my phone interrupts us. It's my ringtone for Meg, and I press my hands against his chest, pushing him away so I can answer.

"Meg?" I try to slow my heart rate, not sure if it's because of JJ, or I'm expecting yet another shoe to drop. "What's up? Is everything okay?"

"Ethan and I are meeting Jon at the skatepark. Don't try to talk me out of it."

"That's a terrible idea."

"I never said it was a good one, but I'm taking backup, so sit tight, and I'll let you know how it goes as soon as we're done."

I feel like I'm going to explode. "This could be a trap, a media stunt. Jon Baker is a legitimate student at Carver High School, but I haven't found out much about him or his mom yet. We need to wait until we have more information."

"Too late. Ethan and I are already heading there. Don't worry, Justice Greystone and his friend, Tony Gerard, are with us. We've got it covered."

I'm totally blown away. My little sister has just outmaneuvered me and called in the big guns. She hangs up before I can say anything else and I stare at my cell, dumbfounded.

"What is it?" JJ asks.

Meg seems to be acting more like me than her. Guess that's what happens when I go down in flames—she has to step up. "I think I've created a monster."

20

Meg

I think I've lost my mind.

That's the only thing on my mind as I walk out of the drugstore, DNA test in hand. My sister's voice rings in my head as I anticipate the brutal lecture she'll give me.

I'll probably melt from her wrath.

And I'd deserve it.

Giving Jon, a fifteen-year-old, a DNA test without parental consent is horrible. I know better. My conscience screams it.

And, yet, here I am.

Meg, Warrior Princess.

Or Idiot Princess.

If Jon is the real Ethan Havers and this case goes to trial, the test—the ultimate piece of evidence—will get thrown out and a kidnapper might go free.

No doubt.

Maybe, if he's still employed, JJ will do his magic and

somehow win a motion to keep it, but there's no counting on that.

As I walk toward my van, I glance at Ethan in the passenger's seat, the late afternoon sun shining on his dark hair and a stab to my midsection rocks me. He looks like every other adolescent kid who should be out trying to lose his virginity. Instead he's sifting through the rubble of his broken world.

That's all I need to shut my conscience up. This is about him and his right to know where he came from.

We've been so busy trying to find Carl and Lily's biological son we've all but abandoned our original assignment of finding out who Ethan is.

He deserves answers.

And if we can connect Jon to Carl or Lily, maybe, just maybe, it'll somehow tie back to Ethan's real parents.

I don't know. One step at a time.

After meeting Jon, if nothing new develops, I'll see how Matt's doing on the list Jerry gave us. Somewhere on it might be Ethan's biological father. Or at least a relative.

I hop in, drop my tote behind Ethan's seat and shove the bag in the console.

"What's that?"

"That, my friend, is a DNA test."

I don't need to look at Ethan to know he's staring at me with those inquisitive eyes that've seen way more than a kid his age should. He's a smart boy and doesn't ask who it's for. Testing Jon's DNA is the obvious step.

Refusing to look at him, I turn the key and make quick work of pulling out of the parking lot. "I'm going to swab him and see if Charlie can get the lab to run the test."

"He's a minor. You need consent."

"What's your point?"

"Whoa! You're kinda badass."

If only.

I shrug and blow through a yellow light. "I have nothing to lose. I'm a sculptor, not a cop. If we get a match on Jon, we'll have at least found..." Lord, how to say this?

"The real Ethan," Ethan adds.

Another light flashes to red and I'm forced to stop. I sit for a second while the silence lingers, forcing me to think when all I want is to not do that. I finally glance at Ethan who has no idea who the hell he is.

"If he's a match, we'll have found Carl and Lily's biological son. *You* will always be Ethan." I smile. "Unless you change your name to Waldo or something equally compelling."

He snorts and the sound bursts the tension like an arrow through a balloon. Relief washes over me and I ease out a breath. This is one great kid.

The light flips to green and I punch the gas. "Ethan, whatever happens with Jon, I promise you, we'll find your father and mother."

Is it fair to make such a bold promise? Who knows? But we owe him that much. I won't give up on him and neither will Charlie. No matter how *delicate* the situation with the Havers.

Who am I kidding? It's a fucking nightmare. I can't see them putting Ethan out though. Even if Carl did show up with a suitcase and allow Ethan to stay with me a couple days while he settled his lunatic wife down.

The man isn't a monster. At least I don't think he is. My take is he's trying to limit Ethan's exposure to his wife's emotional chaos.

Lily? Definitely a monster.

"Yeah," Ethan says. "I know. You guys are awesome."

Whatever mistakes Carl and Lily have made, they've raised an extraordinary young man. For that, I'll give them credit.

I hang a left onto a side street that my GPS tells me should lead to the park. On the sidewalk, two boys riding skateboards head the same direction.

Getting close.

Ethan points straight. "It's on the next block."

"Yep. Here we go, kid."

Two minutes later, I pull into an empty spot across from the park. Row homes line both sides, encircling the quaint wooded play area and a concrete jungle of ramps and rails where a group of teenagers make death-defying jumps—are they nuts?

Surrounding the entire area are benches and a few tables. Sitting at one is a man eating. He's in a dark suit and looks like any other businessman taking a dinner break before heading home. In reality, it's Justice Greystone, a man in charge of some secret group of renegade agents we think is tied to the FBI.

Another of Grey's agents, Tony, should also be out there, but from this vantage point, I can't see him.

Doesn't matter. Their presence settles me and my shoulders instantly drop. If any press managed to follow me, Grey and Tony will deal with them.

This, I know.

I kill the engine, grab my tote and shove the drugstore purchase into it before exiting.

Ethan meets me on the sidewalk and points to the north end of the park. "I told him we'd meet him by the see-saw."

A cold wind whips right through me, making me shiver. I shove my hands in my pockets as we walk the concrete path leading to the playground.

I don't see any teenagers hanging around the benches, but that doesn't mean anything. Jon could be watching for us.

"Meg?"

"Yeah?"

"I'm freaking out a little."

Again, I feel a punch of anxiety for him. "Of course you are. You're about to meet a kid that's possibly...well...you. Charlie is the shrink in our family, but I'd imagine this situation comes with a whole lot of confusion. As long as you keep talking about it and letting the people you care about know how you're feeling, you'll always have help. Your parents love you, Ethan. You know they do."

"Yeah. I know. This is just...weird."

It sure was. "It is. And, look, we're not family, but you can always call me. Or Charlie. Or Matt." I do my best at a winning smile. "We're a full-service agency."

Ethan bumps me with his shoulder. He's more than half my age, but has at least three inches on me and we both laugh at the awkwardness of his action.

"We've got this," Ethan says.

"You bet we do."

Ahead, the scrape of a skateboard draws my eye left. A shaggy haired teenager wheels in and heads straight for the see-saw.

Here we go.

He's tall. Lean. And...dammit, his hair is the exact color of Carl's.

My stomach pitches then rolls. Ethan faces me, his eyes big and focused in a spaced-out way I haven't seen on him before.

I reach for his arm and squeeze. "Let's not jump to conclusions. Don't assume anything. People look like a lot of people. Trust me. I'm a sculptor."

People look like a lot of people? I'm not even sure what the hell that means. I shake it off, chalk it up to nerves.

We turn back and find him settling in on the bench.

Ethan stops. Just halts right in the middle of the path.

"Ethan, we don't have to do this. We can turn and walk right out of here."

For a few seconds he doesn't move. Just stands there staring at Jon. Whatever he decides, I'll support him. As bad as I'd like answers about Jon, I'd walk away.

If it helped Ethan, I'd do it.

But my partner on this mission shakes his head. "No. We have to. If he's the real Ethan, we should help him."

My heart swells. The life he's known has literally crumbled and all he can think about is giving someone else closure.

"Lord, Ethan, you're one heck of a human being. I'm proud to know you."

He hits me with a smile that flashes his perfect teeth. "Thanks, Meg. That's cool."

As we draw closer, Jon stands. He's an inch or two taller than Ethan and I study his features. The cut of his cheekbones, the strong jaw and full mouth.

My pulse hammers, drowning out the sounds of tweeting birds and rustling leaves.

If this kid isn't a Havers, I'm burning my sketch pad.

Has to be.

Jon forces a weak smile. I'm an adult and have no idea how to handle this situation. How is a hormone enraged teenager supposed to?

I glance at Ethan, who squares his shoulders and takes a breath. He picks up his pace, leaving me half a step behind. I hook my hand around the strap of my tote, squeezing hard enough to crinkle the plastic bag tucked inside. My mind snaps to the DNA kit and potential introductions to that little surprise.

Hey, Jon. I know we just met but can I swab your cheek?

It sounds like a pick-up line from a bad B movie.

Too much thinking. I have to stop. Just focus on my one task. The sample. That's it.

Twenty yards away, Grey glances at us then goes back to his sandwich.

I quicken my steps to catch Ethan, who is already a few feet from Jon. "Jon?"

He bobs his head. "Yeah. Hey, Ethan."

The two do a fist bump, shuffle their feet, stare off at the park and then finally, having nothing else to stall with, turn to me as if I'll somehow save them.

I shove my hand out. "Hi, Jon. Nice to meet you. I'm Meg."

He gives me a good, solid handshake that impresses me. "Hey. You're helping Ethan?"

"Yes. Me and my sister, Charlie."

"Yeah. Okay. So, uh, how do we do this? I mean, figure out who I am?"

Bam.

A total gift has just landed at my feet. I pull the bag out. "Well, Jon. I have an idea that'll settle this whole thing."

21

Charlie

*A*t seven the next morning, I'm waiting for Chuck McAllister in the parking lot of Family Ties. It's nestled in a quiet suburb of D.C., birds singing in the nearby park and residents commuting to their jobs on the busy street out front.

Chuck's the supervisor of the lab—they do dozens of DNA analyses every day for paying customers, and have a great reputation in the community here. Every year they hold a reunion for anyone who's used their services to locate lost relatives. It's a huge event, and people travel from all over to attend.

I'm not a paying customer and I don't have consent for testing Jon's DNA. Chuck doesn't need to know it's for a minor, and he owes me a big favor.

He'll still balk, but I'm not feeling congenial today. When Meg starts acting more crazy than usual, I take it seriously. I've already chewed her out, and she's sitting in the car next to me, quietly stewing. I drum my fingers on the steering wheel, feeling too light on sleep and too heavy on caffeine and anxiety.

JJ and I stayed up all night working on different leads. Anita's report came up clean—too clean. When I crosschecked her with her employment history, education, and credit history, I hit dead ends on all three. My time with the Bureau taught me that's a huge red flag, pointing to someone disappearing from their old life and starting over.

In this day and age, you don't get far with a fake ID unless you put some serious cash behind it to pay for premium services. Obtaining a scannable one, like a license, isn't difficult, but creating a background legend that passes serious scrutiny is tough.

The kid's is even more sparse, which wouldn't be unusual due to his age, except for the fact I could find no match in any database to a Jon, born to Anita Baker, with his social security number under the date of birth he supplied to Meg along with his cheek swab.

The birthday could be false, but if so, that's just the tip of the iceberg. Anita is hiding something—and I have that tickle in my chest that tells me it's big.

I sent the information to Matt in order to share it with Taylor and get her onboard. She has access to a few more databases than I do, although a lot less time, to hunt down this lead. She's focused on finding Ethan's real parents.

My phone signals an incoming call. ID reads Lily Havers.

What does she want? An interview so she can rake me over the coals again on air?

"Who is it?" Meg asks.

"No one."

She takes the phone from my hand. "By the scowl on your face, I doubt that." Seeing the name, she gives me big eyes. "You've got to be kidding."

It goes to voicemail. I drum my fingers. A moment later, my phone pings, telling me there's a message.

Oh goodie.

Meg ignores my request not to listen to it. At least she doesn't put it on speaker, but when she turns to look at me, goosebumps form on my skin.

I reach over and take the phone away. I only hear the end, so I press the play button again.

Lily demands that we allow her to see Ethan. There's a lot more flourish to it than that, complete with some choice name-calling, but that's the gist of it.

I delete the message and set the phone back in the cup holder.

This morning, I'm running with the DNA that my feisty younger sister copped from Jon. In the backseat, Ethan and JJ share breakfast sandwiches and coffee, the boy now leaning his head on the window, eyes drooping as he finishes his food. From what Meg said, he didn't get much sleep. He's got earbuds in, but even so, the music from his playlist is loud enough for me to hear.

The rattle of the fast food bag grates on my nerves as JJ crumples it behind my seat. I lift my gaze to meet his in the rearview mirror just as Chuck's electric car pulls into the nearly empty parking lot at 7:03.

My brain is humming, my blood, too. I didn't plan to bring everybody, but I didn't have any choice when they all piled into my BMW. This is the only thing any of us have right now, so even though we're all exhausted, and maybe a little scared, we're here. Every one of us is supporting the other, a makeshift family with little else left to lose and everything to gain as we stick together come hell or high water.

"Everybody stay put," I say, grabbing the drugstore bag. Amazing how accessible these things are anymore. "I'll be right back."

Nobody argues––must be a first. Drawing my shoulders back, I leave the car and stride to meet Chuck as he's unlocking the back door to the lab.

He hears my heels clicking across the pavement and glances over his shoulder at me. "Charlie Schock," he says, surprised. "You're up early. Something I can do for you?"

I give him a professional smile, too tired to really pour on the charm, and besides, Chuck swore off women after his divorce. "Yes, actually. I have a special request."

The welcoming expression turns wary. "Must be very special if you're here in person."

I hear a door slam behind me and see Meg on her way to join us. I fight the urge to roll my eyes. Of course, she couldn't stay in the car.

Ignoring her, I decide I might have to nip this argument in the bud before Chuck has a chance to start it. I hold up the bag. "I need an analysis ASAP and it's an extremely delicate situation, so I came straight to you. I can't trust this with just anyone—"

His eyes shutter and he raises a hand. "Look, Charlie, I saw the news. If this has anything to do with that kid"—he shakes his head—"I'm not getting within two miles of that."

I push my sunglasses to the top of my head, so I can look him in the eye. "This is strictly off the books. I will pay in full in cash right now, no questions asked, and your name will never be associated with the test."

Another head shake. He eyes Meg. "You know I can't get involved unless you go through proper channels."

"Can't or won't?" Meg asks. Her posture is relaxed, but she's shooting daggers at him, and in her current state of pissed-off-edness, she looks like she's ready to go for his jugular.

Chuck opens the door, ready to bolt and lock us out. "I'd like to help, really, but there's no way I can do anything under the table, and with all the media coverage? If Family Ties became associated with this, we'd be in a shitstorm. Our reputation could get severely damaged. It could cost me my job."

Yep, I figured this was where we would end up. My pulse is slamming, my foot itching to tap on the blacktop—or maybe kick him in the shins. Funny how stress can cause you to resort to childish behavior. I should've just started with my threat—would've made this whole process faster and easier.

"Listen, Chuck, the last thing I want to do is create trouble for you or Family Ties. We've done a lot of good work together, helping people find relatives and be reunited with their families, but here's the deal—I've done tons of free marketing and promotion for you guys with my ancestry clients and never asked for a dime in return. Now, my back is against the wall, and I need help. Kind of like the time you called me when your now ex-wife was banging a female stripper and Mayor Hennessey's wife at the same time, and failed to mention to you she was gay." Calling up my cocky Charlie façade, I wink at Meg, my co-conspirator. "As I recall, I got you what you needed for a speedy and not-so-costly divorce. In short, you owe me."

I don't have to spell out the rest—if he's worried about reputations, that story could ruin both of their's, thanks to his ex. It could also cause our mayor political ruin. I would never actually reveal anything like that, but Chuck doesn't know it.

One of Meg's eyebrows lifts, a faint smile passing over her lips as she sees my blackmail for what it is. She pulls her phone out of her pocket and acts like she's dialing. "Matt's at the office standing by, ready to release the information to Channel 4 News." She glances at Chuck. "Your call."

His eyes bounce wildly between us, fearful and incredulous at the same time. "Now wait. Let's not do anything hasty here."

Gotcha. I hold up the bag again, smiling. "We'll wait. Text me when you're done."

With a dramatic sigh, accompanied by an eyeroll, he

snatches it from my hand. "It'll be at least twenty-four hours. I can't go any faster than that."

I hand him a copy of Carl's DNA analysis. "These are the markers we're looking for. You have twenty minutes."

"The machine doesn't work that fast, Charlie," he whines. "You know that."

I know he'll need at least a couple hours, due to that very fact, but putting pressure on him is important. Once inside, he might get cold feet or be distracted.

I point to my car. "We'll be over there. If I don't hear from you within two hours, I'm coming in to run the damn thing myself, and if I have to come in there, everyone's going to know why, and Meg is making that call. Do we understand each other?"

He sets his jaw, gives me a curt nod, and disappears.

Meg and I look at each other as the door slams shut. She raises her fist and I bump it.

As we walk back, her phone rings. "It's Matt," she informs me.

Inside the car, she puts him on speaker.

"Two things," he says. The tone of his voice makes the tickle in my chest kick up a notch. "First, I spoke to a guy on the list this morning, named George Olsen, who said he got a woman pregnant in California sixteen years ago. Santa Monica. George claims it was a one-night stand, he wasn't ready to be a father, they had no desire to get married, yada, yada, yada. She told him she was going to terminate the pregnancy. He doesn't know if she did or not; they went their separate ways. He's agreed to do a DNA test."

At least it's something. If the woman had the baby and gave him up for adoption...I glance back at Ethan, now sleeping with his earphones still in and the music blasting away. "Did George give you her name?"

"Couldn't remember it. Thinks she went by Raven or some

other bird name, but he doubted it was real. I'm doing a search for anyone who might fit."

"What else?"

"Taylor is totally working her ass off, but she doesn't have time to do all the nitty-gritty research we need so I hit up Grey and Teeg. Teeg was able to trace the social security number Anita is using for Jon back to a guy who died in World War I. Definite identity theft. The best news? You better sit down for this."

I nearly rip the phone out of Meg's hand. "What is it, Matt?"

"He got a facial recognition hit from the picture on Anita's license. Looks like she may have had plastic surgery, but there are two markers that match—her eyes and earlobes."

JJ sits forward, gripping my seat. "And?"

"If this is the same gal, she may actually be Susie Norris."

My pulse slams so hard in my throat, I can barely speak. "You mean she's related to Amelia, the Havers' kidnapper?"

His next words send chills down my spine. "Sisters probably, although I haven't verified that yet. Looks like they lived together here in D.C. fifteen years ago, according to a rental agreement under Amelia's name that I dug up. Right before that, guess where they lived?"

I don't have to think twice. "Santa Monica, California."

"Give the lady a prize."

"Holy shit." Meg does a fist pump in the air. "We've got a real lead."

I turn the key and throw the car into drive. Susie, aka Anita, may have already left for work at the accountant's office where she has a job. "We're going to see her," I tell Matt.

"You need her address?" he asks.

"I've got it from the background check I did last night. Keep looking for George's girlfriend and see if Taylor will do a search for missing kids in California, especially any in Santa Monica that fit our parameters. George's one-night stand may have had the baby and given it up for adoption, or it was kidnapped just like Ethan."

"I'm on it."

Meg disconnects and we hit the highway, heading for another suburb and Anita's home.

22

Meg

I'm freaking out.

We're racing to Anita's house with Ethan and JJ in tow and every ounce of me is rebelling. Ethan has been through enough and we have no idea what we're subjecting him to.

And then there's JJ. Should he be here? On a professional level, I have no idea what kind of conflict this represents. He's on suspension but he's still a U.S. attorney.

Charlie hits the expressway ramp going fifty and presses the gas while I grip the door handle.

"I think we should drop JJ and Ethan at the office."

"I'm going," JJ adds.

"Me, too."

I spin back to JJ. "Have you lost your mind?"

He gives me a rueful smile. "Probably long ago."

"Well," Charlie says, "Ethan is a kid. We're the adults. He

shouldn't be here."

"Hey," the so-called kid says. "It's my life. And, I'm the one who came to you in the first place."

I glance at my sister whose eyes haven't left the road. A good thing since she's pushing eighty-five.

"Charlie?" Ethan asks. "Please."

He's a charmer. Charlie's right, he shouldn't be here, but he's not your average teenager. He's already seen too much of life. Plus, he's been involved from the get-go.

Charlie sneaks a peek in the rearview and meets JJ's eye. "Damn you, both. Promise me you'll stay in the car."

"Nuh-uh. No way." This from Ethan.

I turn back to JJ, silently pleading. We don't know what we'll be walking into and we have to protect him. Even if he's been an active part of this investigation, some lines we can't cross.

JJ nods. "We'll stay in the car."

"That's crap," Ethan whines.

Relief settles on me and I let out a long breath. "Yeah, well, welcome to life, my young friend."

We spend the next twenty minutes ensconced in blessed quiet, but I know my sister. She's devising a plan. I can see it in the set of her jaw, her focus on the road.

She's in takedown mode.

Look out, people.

Ethan's phone buzzes. "It's my dad," he says.

As promised, Ethan has been sticking to the deal of checking in with Carl every hour and I'm thankful he hasn't wavered. Arguing with a teenager, on top of everything else, might require a couple extra pot brownies.

We arrive in Hyattsville, Maryland, and cruise through a quaint downtown area filled with art centers and studios. Any other day, I'd grab a coffee, take in the scene and feed my creative soul.

Today? No time.

The GPS directs Charlie to make a left, then a quick right onto a street with craftsman homes and bungalows, some in desperate need of TLC. Chipped paint, crumbling brick and overgrown shrubs and weeds abound, but oh, the potential here.

"Slow down," I say. "We're getting close. It's the blue one."

Two doors down on our right, a woman rushes down the sagging porch of a cornflower blue bungalow. She's carrying a large green garbage bag, clearly heading to the car in the gravel driveway. The trunk is open and my pulse kicks up.

Jon, the boy we met with at the skate park, shoves open the screen door, waving his arms as he chases after the woman.

Charlie hits the brakes, parks under a tree and pops her own trunk.

What is she up to now? "What are you doing?"

"I have a parabolic mic."

Crap. "Is that legal?"

"Do we care?"

She hops out, sticking close to the car.

"I'm not hearing this," JJ comments.

"Wait," Ethan says. "I got a text. From Jon."

I whip around and watch as he reads it.

"His mom is wigging out. They're going to Minnesota."

What the hell?

In seconds Charlie is back, handing me a mini-satellite dish looking thing that's about twelve inches tall. She fiddles with her handheld recorder then plugs a set of headphones into it. Snatching the dish from me she connects the devices.

"They're going to Minnesota," I tell her.

"Why?"

"We don't know. Jon just texted Ethan."

"Let's find out." She punches a button and slips her headphones on. "Everyone, ssshhh."

We all obey while she points toward Anita and Jon, gently sweeping it back and forth.

At the house, Anita runs back inside, her hands flying as her mouth moves. I'm dying to ask what they're talking about, but I know better. My sister will tear me a new one if I say anything and cause her to miss something.

Charlie looks at me. "New position in Minnesota. She's claiming he'll love it there."

"What job?"

"Ssshh."

She jerks her chin to the windshield. Anita and Jon are out front again, Jon chasing her down while he holds his hands out in front of him. He reaches for her, spinning her around.

"Dang," Charlie says. "He's absolutely begging her to stay."

This poor kid. She's ripping him from his home, friends, school. I peer out and think about my childhood, thankful for the normalcy that came with it. My bed, the river. Even our nutty mother trying to prove our oddball neighbor was up to something illegal. All of it floods back to me, reminding me I lived an ideal life.

Anita points to the passenger side of her beat-up sedan, but Jon is having none of it. He steps back, folding his arms across his chest. A dug in teenager. Anita might be screwed.

If they get into that car, we might be, too.

I reach for the door handle, yanking on it.

Charlie latches onto my arm. "What are you *doing*?"

"I don't know. But I can't sit here. This woman might have answers."

"I'm going, too."

Ethan again. This time, I'm the one dug in. I whip around, poking my finger at him. "No! Don't move. Do you hear me?"

Charlie hits a button on her door. "He's not going anywhere." She grins. "Child locks."

Behind her, JJ snorts. "You two are a pisser."

"Well, this pisser is going out there. I'm gonna stall her. We can't let them leave until we get that DNA test back."

Charlie sets the recording contraption in her lap. "I'll call Taylor. See if they can help."

I hustle from the car, thankful for Anita's distraction with Jon as they face-off on the neglected lawn.

Eventually, she'll notice me. No matter how preoccupied she may be, she'll spot me in her peripheral vision.

Like...now.

She angles toward me, gives me the hard stare of suspicion and slides in front of Jon. Whatever she's done, I'll give her credit for protective instincts.

"May I help you?"

I probably should've thought this out before approaching because I'm at a loss as to what to say. And somehow, I don't think accusing her of kidnapping will get us off on the right foot.

Pretending to be a bible salesman is out so I go to plan H. "Susie Norris?"

Her hard stare slowly disintegrates and her eyes drift wide. Slowly, her mouth parts. She rocks back then immediately straightens and my head nearly explodes from the blood rush.

Apparently, no one has called her that in a long time.

I keep walking, heading straight for her now with less than twenty feet to go. "Do you remember me? How the heck are you?"

Behind her, Jon peers over her shoulder. Hopefully, he'll keep his mouth shut and let me do my thing.

"Sorry," she says. "There's no one here by that name."

She angles back to Jon. "Get in the car. We're going."

I close the distance between us and stop just far enough from her to ward off any kind of attack she might initiate. "Susie, I need to talk to you."

"Look, I just told you. I'm not Susie." She turns and opens

the passenger side door. "Get in, Jon. I mean it."

When she blasts him with a look, the kid relents and slides in.

No. Please no.

Another burst slams inside my head sending simultaneous bolts through my limbs.

I can't let them go. No way. She's already lived for years under a fake identity. If they leave now, who knows how long they'll be underground.

From behind me, a car door slams. Has to be Charlie. Excellent. She'll know what to do. While Susie heads to the other side, I peek at my approaching sister.

"Hello," she calls. "Anita?"

Susie/Anita's head whips around, her gaze pinging from me to Charlie. Me to Charlie. Me to Charlie.

Whoopsie.

Should've definitely coordinated with big sis on this one. We've just blown our hand and my breath quickens. Do something. *Stop them.*

My vision blurs from the adrenaline storming my system and I force a breath. If I don't get myself under control, the panic attack will take me down.

No.

Susie picks up her pace, rips the door open and guns the engine.

In seconds, they'll be out of the driveway and by the time Charlie and I get back to the car, they could be gone.

Gone, gone.

My skin is absolutely on fire as I look at Charlie, still a good thirty feet away. No help there. The sound of Susie's transmission shifting gears drowns the chaos in my head. She's going. Right now. Taking Jon and leaving.

I do the only thing I can.

I jump into Susie's backseat.

23

Charlie

"*W*hat the ever livin'...?"

I'm so stunned at what I just saw, I don't react for a heartbeat.

Then I wish I had my gun.

To shoot Anita's tire and stop her from running away. Or maybe my sister for her fool brain, knee-jerk reaction.

Better yet, myself for putting us in this situation in the first place.

I haul ass, running alongside the car down the block, as if I can somehow stop Anita—Susie—with my bare hands. I yell and pound at her driver side window, ignoring her grim determination not to look at me, the fear I see in Jon's eyes, and the fact my sister is reaching forward from the backseat to grab the woman's shoulder.

Susie hits the gas and no matter how hard I run, I can't keep up. I stand in the middle of the road, raise both hands and scream my lungs out for three seconds.

An engine revs behind me. JJ.

Bless him all to pieces.

He shoots up next to me, slams on the brakes and throws open the passenger door. "Get in!"

I'm halfway into the seat when he takes off, the inertia slamming my door shut. I strike the dashboard over and over again with my fist as we give chase. "What the hell is she thinking?"

"It's Meg," JJ replies, as if this explains everything.

It does, actually.

Ethan grips the back of my seat, leveraging himself forward to watch as we streak through suburbia. I wish I was a fly inside Susie's sedan and could hear what Meg's saying to her.

I call Matt and alert him we're no longer at the residence and give him the general direction we're headed—to the highway. He tells me Taylor, as well as Grey and Tony, are all on the way and he'll redirect them. In my gut, I know they won't get here in time to help us.

"We just have to stay with her until Taylor can catch up," I tell JJ.

"Jon is totally freaking out," Ethan says. They're texting.

"Tell him to stay calm and make sure he has a seatbelt on. Ask him to keep us posted if he can about what's going on. Did he say what Meg is doing?"

Ethan falls silent, and I know he's asking Jon. I glance over my shoulder. "Get your seatbelt on," I order.

He manages to complete his text and roll his eyes at the same time, before sliding back and following my instructions. "Jon says she's talking to his mom. Does she really think she can run away and kidnap Jon again?"

That's exactly what she's trying to do. "Not if I can help it."

"She's not going anywhere," JJ reassures both of us with a

tone I know well. "I alerted the local PD and gave them her plate number. Even if we lose her, she won't get far."

Susie blows through a red light and I suck in my breath. Thank God traffic is minimal. People are already at work, the kids at school. JJ slows, checks both directions, and since nothing's coming, speeds up again.

We're losing ground though, and I'm grinding my teeth to keep from yelling at him to speed up. Car chases through suburban neighborhoods aren't recommended, but if we let Susie get on the highway, my sister's life—as well as Jon's—could be in even more danger.

24

Meg

*W*hat have I done?

I'm sitting in Susie's car squeezing the handle like it's a rope saving me from a rogue wave.

"Susie!" I yell. "For God's sake, slow down before you kill us all."

She's just torn through a red light and narrowly missed being clipped by a truck. If it had been moving any faster, Jon and I would be toast.

Why I thought jumping in with this maniac was wise, I have no idea.

I'm also kidding myself. When would I ever let a young man —a teenager—be kidnapped without trying to help?

"Shut up." Susie switches lanes, bullying in between two vehicles, pounding on her horn. "Get out of the way! Move it."

"Mom!" Jon cries. "Please. Stop!"

I slide my phone out, ready to dial nine-one-one just as she zigs back. Momentum jerks it from my hand, sends it tumbling to the floorboard.

Dammit.

I lean left, but Suzie picks then to play slalom with three other cars and I'm rocked right, slamming my head against the closed window.

Forget the phone. I'm liable to wind up with a concussion or a cracked skull.

I straighten, looking for Charlie's BMW. My sister must be cursing me right now. A lecture is sure to follow, but I can't worry about that.

"Susie," I say, closing my eyes again as the approaching light switches to amber. "Please, just pull over. Let Jon out. Keep me if you want, but he doesn't deserve this."

"He's my son," she says. "He's not going anywhere."

"You're willing to let him die? That truck back there nearly crashed into us."

I peek and see the light is now red.

Ohmygod. Anticipating the inevitable, I dip my head. *Please, God, please.* My body tenses, everything squeezed so tight my shoulders and neck cramp.

Horns blare again, a noise I'm becoming way too comfortable with on this ride from hell.

"Mom! That was close."

I open my eyes just as Susie clears the intersection. Behind me the squeal of brakes sounds, then the crunch of metal. I spin, see two mangled cars in the intersection, airbags deployed.

"You better hope those people are all right," I say. "Or you're going to jail for that alone."

Never mind the other crimes she's committed. At this point, she'll be lucky to get out of prison before she dies of old age.

"Shut up," she tells me again.

As if that worked the first time. Not a chance. Obviously, I'm irritating her. Which, may or may not be a good thing right now. All I know is I have to help Jon.

"Pull over. Let Jon out and I'll shut up. Then you and I take off. Don't be stupid. If you love him, you'll let him go. Don't make him die in this car."

"If I do, so does he."

A car makes a right on red, zipping in front of us.

"Mom! Watch it!"

Susie cuts the wheel left, darting into the other lane and punching the gas again making a straightaway out of the main thoroughfare.

"Jon, stop that yelling. I can't think."

"Mom," he says, his voice unsteady and tight. "Please, let me out. I'm...scared."

Oh, this kid. He's destroying me.

In the distance, I hear sirens. Whether they're for us, I don't know, but I swivel my head back and forth, sweeping my gaze along the road where fast food restaurants and mom-and-pop stores line both sides.

We shoot by a corner gas station and I glance down the intersecting road. Police car. Couple blocks down.

The cavalry is on the way.

I just have to hope we don't get killed before they reach us.

25

Charlie

We speed by a gas station, hair salon, and dentist. "Can we cut her off before she reaches the highway?" I yell at JJ.

He's gritting his teeth, hands white-knuckling the wheel. "No. All we can do is follow."

My phone rings.

"Yeah. A little busy here, Taylor."

"We're on our way. Do not engage, Charlie. Let us handle this."

I want to, I do, but there's no way Taylor will get to Susie before we do. "She's got Meg."

"I know, but this is a federal investigation you're messing in."

"And you're still a dozen blocks from her house. I'm right on her tail. If you're going to catch her before I do, you'll have to hurry."

I end the conversation and JJ shakes his head. "Are you

trying to piss off the one person in your corner besides me and Meg?"

"And me," Ethan calls. "And Jon."

"If a little friendly competition will get her here faster," I tell JJ, "I'll suffer the consequences."

I get a text from Matt saying he's six blocks behind us. Grey and Tony are a mile away, coming in from the east. If we can slow Susie down and surround her, we'll have a chance to force her off the road in a controlled manner, so she doesn't hurt anybody.

She takes a sharp right, tires squealing. JJ stays on her tail, and I have to grab the dash to keep from falling over.

"Put on *your* seatbelt, Charlie," Ethan gripes at me.

Smart alec. But I do as he says then text Meg. *Be safe, little sister. We don't know if she's violent. Try to get her to pull over and let you out.*

Three blocks down, JJ has to jerk the wheel to get around a truck backing out of a driveway. Ahead, Susie takes a left and disappears from sight.

There's no return text from Meg, but I didn't expect one. As we finally get to the turn, I look ahead and my stomach bottoms out.

They've disappeared.

I curse under my breath, then my training kicks in hard. Everything inside me goes very still. As we fly down the block passing a set of small businesses on the right, I happen to catch sight of the sedan in an alley.

"Wait!" I yell at JJ. "Back up!"

He doesn't argue, and I nearly get whiplash from the sudden stop before he throws the BMW in reverse. Just as we reach the opening, I see the bumper disappearing out the other end. "There." I point.

JJ wheels us down the alley, my car's rear fishtailing and banging into a dumpster. Flying down the narrow passageway, we follow, and then go left, finding ourselves in a large shopping center's parking lot.

There are rows of cars everywhere I look, even though there's a considerable amount of empty spaces. We'll never find them in here, unless we scan up and down all of them.

"Dammit." I bang my fist on the dashboard. "Where did they disappear to?"

Susie could've driven through the lot and around the back of another store, for all I know.

Ethan sits forward again. His finger shoots out near my shoulder. "There! Jon said they're behind that delivery van by the building."

At the far side, the furniture store has multiple trucks. There are a dozen cars parked near them, probably employees.

JJ slips in beside a four-wheel drive pickup where we can partially see the backside of Susie's car. I'm already texting the address to Matt, who'll share it with Taylor, Grey, and Tony.

"Sit tight. We don't want to scare her off again," JJ says.

The last thing I want to do is sit here, helpless. I wish I knew Meg was okay—she still hasn't answered. "What's Jon saying now?" I ask Ethan.

"His mom is arguing with Meg. Charlie?"

I glance at him. "What?"

His eyes are big in his face. "There's no way this woman is *my* real mother, right?"

Poor kid. For a second, I consider telling him I'm not sure, but what good will that do? He needs hope as much as I do right now. "It sounds like Susie and her sister, Amelia, kidnapped you and Jon both. Most likely, your mom is still out there, and we'll find her, I promise."

Sirens blare in the distance. I don't know if they're coming for Susie or someone else.

A car door flings open, and Jon bails out. He starts heading our direction and I whip around to look at Ethan again. "Did you tell him we were here?"

He just looks back at me, the answer in his eyes. "I told him to get the hell out as soon as he could and you'd protect him."

It hits me right in the breastbone. That this kid has so much faith in me when I let him and everyone else down.

"How do you want to handle this, Charlie?" JJ asks.

Another door flies open and Susie jumps out, screaming at Jon. He picks up his pace and sprints toward us, throwing a scared look back at her.

My heart kicks hard. Where is Meg? *Please let her be okay.*

In the next instant, my sister appears, and I sigh audibly. "There she is."

She's trying to calm Susie, while stepping in front of her to block her from Jon.

I release my belt, open my door, and tell JJ, "Get Jon in the car."

I take off and start running toward Meg and Susie. As Jon and I pass each other, he gives me a frightened look. "Get in the back," I tell him. "You're safe now."

Meg is doing a dance with Susie, trying to keep in front of her as the woman charges, screaming Jon's name at the top of her lungs. The sirens grow closer, and we're drawing notice from people leaving the store.

I speed up, reading Susie's body language, and yep, as I suspected, before I can get there, she grabs Meg and shoves her to the ground.

Meg being Meg, she sticks out her leg and trips the woman. *That's my sister.*

Susie jumps up clumsily, screaming obscenities at her, and me as well. She rushes toward me, anger in her face, fists raised.

I'm not sure if it's a mother's instinct for her child, even though Jon is technically not hers, or if it's just rage at being found out, but she's in bulldozer mode and there's little that'll stop her from getting to the boy unless I do something drastic.

Good thing I don't have my gun.

I stop, and as she comes at me, I wait until she's nearly in my face. She rears back as if to hit me, and I send a right jab straight into her nose.

Her cursing turns into a cry of pain. I feel cartilage crunch under my knuckles and she stumbles, grabbing at her face.

Her feet tangle and she lands on her butt. Rolling on the asphalt, she cries out, blood seeping through her fingers as she cradles her nose.

My knuckles burn, but the adrenaline is flowing and I barely feel it, shaking out my hand and standing over her. "Nobody hurts my sister and gets away with it," I tell her. As if that's the worst of her crimes.

In my book, it pretty much is.

She tries to roll to her hands and knees and I use my foot to push her back down. "If you know what's good for you, you'll stay on the ground."

She curls into a ball, sobbing. I jog over and make sure Meg's okay. She brushes off her jeans and gives me a quick hug. Together we surround Susie, who is still crying and wiping her bloody nose on her sleeve.

"You're Amelia's sister, aren't you?" I ask.

I hear screeching tires and see Matt speeding in. Tony's truck is behind him, Grey in the passenger seat. The sirens are only a block or so away now, and I'm sure they're coming to us.

I pull my cell out and hit my record app. I want a confession before they take her away.

Grabbing Susie by the arm, I haul her into a sitting position. Shoving my phone in her face, I ask again, "Are you Amelia Norris's sister?"

She swipes at her wet cheeks. "What does it matter? She's dead."

"Which one of you kidnapped Jon and Ethan, or were you both involved?"

"I love him. He's mine."

"Who?" Meg asks. "Jon?"

She nods, raising her chin in defiance. "Amelia wanted him for herself, but he bonded with me." She jabs a thumb into her chest. Her sad eyes lock with mine. "I left her the other kid."

"Is Jon the real Ethan Havers?"

She nods, and I repeat the question, wiggling the phone in her face. "Answer verbally."

"I want a lawyer."

I sigh. Matt and Tony join us, stepping up to crowd around Susie. "Are you okay?" Matt asks Meg softly and she nods.

I jab Susie. "Finish answering my questions. Who is the boy that was with Amelia when she killed herself?"

She gives me a hard look. "I don't know. She never told me."

And then through the tears and the blood, she gives me a knowing smile.

She's lying.

It takes a lot of willpower not to slap her. Does she really think she has the upper hand here? That it's okay to play with a young boy's life like this?

"We need to move somewhere else," Matt murmurs to me. "You have an audience."

Glancing around, I see half a dozen people a few feet away, watching the show. One of them is recording it on their cell phone.

Taylor tears into the lot in a big SUV with a light on top. I haul Susie to her feet. "Let's get you that lawyer," I tell her, giving her a tight smile. I want her to know she's going to need more than that to save her ass by the time I'm done with her.

I lean forward and speak quietly into her ear, painting a graphic picture of what will happen to her in federal prison.

Her eyes widen. Then I offer the carrot—if she tells me the truth, I'll make sure the FBI grants her some leniency.

She believes I have that power. I don't dissuade her of the idea.

She puts her mouth close to the phone's speaker. "We kidnapped the boys—me and my sister—because we wanted babies. Except we both wanted Ethan. The boys looked alike, but he was mine. I had to steal him away so I could have him all to myself. I renamed him Jon."

"And the one you left with Amelia? Where did you get him?"

"She kidnapped him from a neighbor when we lived in California. We moved to D.C. and Amelia got hired by the Havers almost right away. She was a registered nurse, you know. She did a lot of babysitting—parents like someone with medical training taking care of their kid. That's how she got close to them. But she only took the babies whose mothers didn't want them."

Matt smiles. "That wasn't so hard now, was it?"

He escorts Susie to Taylor, who's marching our way.

Beck and Jackie are with her. Matt turns Susie over. Meg and I give our statements. I let Taylor listen to Susie's recorded confession and she has me send her a copy.

Susie is placed under arrest. She's screaming for a lawyer as Beck shoves her in the backseat of a police squad car.

Jon—the real Ethan—and Ethan are still in my car, but JJ joins us to put his two cents into the mix, and I finally feel a sense of relief as we explain everything to Taylor. Grey hangs out with Matt, Tony bringing him up to speed.

Jackie pulls me aside. A news crew is pulling in and she drags me behind one of the delivery trucks out of sight. "I've been asked to turn your case over to another lawyer," she says.

"What? Why?"

"Conflict of interest." She points at Beck. "My boyfriend

happens to be one of the agents working on the reopened Havers' case."

She doesn't have to spell it out. In the civil cases Lily is bringing against all of us, the FBI wants to make sure Beck isn't feeding my lawyer information that might help me and damage them. "So you're bailing on me?"

She looks as unhappy as I feel. "I'll text you the name and numbers of several good attorneys I know."

With that she leaves.

My cell chimes. Chuck.

"The results are ready," he says. "Where are you?"

"Are they a match?"

"I can't give out test results over the phone, Charlie, you know that. Especially tests I shouldn't be doing in the first place."

"Yes or no, that's all I need."

"If you want them, come get them."

He hangs up.

Bastard. I grip the phone so tight, I expect to crush it like the Hulk.

Trying to steady my breath, I point Meg to the car where Ethan and Jon still wait. "Let's go. We've got lab results to pick up."

26

Meg

*J*on is Ethan Havers.

For some reason, I'm still having trouble wrapping my mind around it. It's not so much that I don't believe it. I do. I'm simply...shocked.

At this case.

At the last few weeks.

At the two boys whose lives have been thrown into disarray. How will they ever recover?

After leaving Jon and Ethan in the reception area of the lab, Charlie and I sit in Chuck's no-frills, white-walled office as he reviews the analysis with us. JJ had an emergency call from his office and cabbed it to his home so he could access his laptop. Even though he's on suspension, he still has case notes the prosecutors need. And, well, he's JJ.

A good guy and a top-notch lawyer. Most would say 'screw you' to the government.

Chuck, meanwhile, gives us scientific terminology that soars above my head.

From what I can tell, what it comes down to is Jon is a ninety-nine percent match to Carl.

Somehow, I'm not relieved. Yes, a huge ball of pressure has vaporized, but in its wake is the fact we haven't yet found Ethan's real parents. George Olsen's DNA results may change that, but as yet, we don't know.

I sit back and meet my sister's gaze. "We have to tell Jon and Ethan about this. But they're just kids. It doesn't feel right dropping it on them."

"I agree."

"We should tell Carl and Lily first. Right? And probably fess up to Taylor that we—I—obtained a sample from Jon."

Charlie smiles at me, sarcasm all but dripping from her. "Nice try. We're a team."

"Obtaining it was my doing. Why should you go down for it?"

She waves me off. "It won't matter. We got the confession. Besides, the Feds will do another DNA test. And, yes, we should talk to them before we tell the boys. They're the parents. They'll need to decide how they want to handle the situation. For both Jon and Ethan." Charlie shakes her head. "My God. What a cluster."

Chuck clears his throat and stands. "I probably shouldn't be in on this conversation. I'll leave you two alone."

I hold my hand up. "It's okay. I think we're done here."

"We're good." Charlie pushes out of her seat, reaching across the desk to shake Chuck's hand. "Thank you. I know I dragged you into this. I'm sorry for that, but we've done a good thing here. A very good thing."

With that, we say our goodbyes and head toward the lobby where Jon and Ethan are leaning against a wall across from the receptionist's desk, staring off into space.

Whatever is going on in their minds has not only silenced them, it's paralyzed their constant need to be on their phones.

"Let's go, boys," I say.

The two have long faces and droopy eyes and I wonder what it must feel like to know your history has just been rewritten.

Lord, they're just kids. They don't deserve this.

They exchange a look, then turn toward the door.

"Thank you," I tell the older woman behind the desk as we all cruise by her.

We pile into the BMW and everyone buckles up.

"Where are we going now?"

This from Ethan.

A good question. We have two boys, one of whom has been raised by the other's biological parents and those parents don't even know their kidnapped son has been rescued.

I've been in a lot of strange situations. This one?

Trumps them all.

It's almost lunchtime and my stomach actually rumbles. At a loss for what to do next, I point to the burger joint down the road. When all else fails, eat.

"Let's grab some food. Get these boys fed."

Charlie meets my eye for a quick second. "I agree. After that, I think you should take them to your place. The office will be crawling with press. Grey is sending Mitch and Tony to help control it, but I'd like to keep the boys out of sight."

"That works. What about Carl and Lily?"

The minute the words leave my mouth, I regret it. Damn. I shouldn't have even brought them up. The boys don't know the DNA results yet and even mentioning Carl and Lily adds tension that sucks oxygen from the confines of the car.

Or it might just be me because my chest is all locked up. It's as if my respiratory system has imploded.

All I know is I'm strung out and not thinking straight.

"Crap." I force a hard breath, releasing some of the pressure. "It's been a long week today."

I peer out the passenger side window and spot Ethan's reflection in the mirror. He's mouthing something to Jon. What's that about? I whip around and give them a hard stare.

"What are you two up to?"

They exchange another glance, both wearing the wide-eyed look of guilt.

Ethan, always the brave one, lifts his chin. "We know."

I give Charlie a little side eye but she's busy navigating traffic.

With no help coming from my sister, I focus on Ethan again. "What specifically?"

"About the DNA test."

My pulse throbs sending a burst of energy zipping from my head to my heels.

They know.

Impossible. We left them in the lobby when we spoke to Chuck and there was no way they'd learned the results while we were in there.

They might be playing me—us—to see if we'll fall for it. They're resourceful. And sneaky.

No matter how much I like Ethan, I wouldn't put it past him to con me for intel.

Forget the side eye. I full-on turn my head to Charlie. She's the headshrinker in this dynamic duo. Maybe she knows what to do.

My sister remains silent.

"Gee," I say. "My hero."

I turn back, once again giving the boys my best tell-me-or-die look. "What do you know? One of you better start talking."

A few seconds in, Jon lifts a shoulder, lets it drop. "We know I'm the real Ethan Havers."

My pulse continues to brutalize me. *Pound, pound, pound.* The pressure drains me, makes my thoughts fuzzy.

They know. How?

Bluffing.

They have to be. I'm not falling for it. No way.

"Well, I don't know what you think you know—"

"We listened in by the door."

Oh.

Shit.

Charlie whips into the burger joint and slams the car into park before whirling in her seat. "How? We left you with the receptionist. She wouldn't just let you wander around."

Clearly unafraid of Charlie's bitchy tone, Jon straightens. "We watched you go into that guy's office so we said we had to take a piss."

Ethan nods. "Yeah. We were polite and told her we'd both go so we wouldn't get lost. We were all 'we'll be quick, we promise. We just really have to pee. Please?' She went for it and gave us visitors' passes. On the way there, we heard Charlie's voice and eavesdropped."

These boys. Unbelievable. It shouldn't surprise me though. From the start, Ethan has been wily. I collapse, resting the side of my head against the cushion. Not a break to be had here and between the serial killer case and now this, I'm beyond exhausted. Mentally and physically.

I have to shake this off though. We have two teenagers in limbo and they deserve better from me. I lift my head and peer over the seat at the boys.

An odd burst of pride anchors me. They aren't my family, but I couldn't be prouder.

"Before we say anything else, you both need to know you're remarkable young men. Most kids would be acting like...well... assholes...right now."

Ethan lets out a snort. "Language, Meg."

I smile at him and we share a laugh. One day, I hope to have a son like him. Smart and funny and level-headed.

Jerome's question seeps back to me, nudging me in a direction that terrifies me.

I could have a good life with him. A great life.

With kids.

I love him. At least, I think I do. I know I can't lose him. That would wreck me. When this is over, I owe him an answer.

For now, I slide my pointed finger between the young men. "What did you hear?"

"I'm a ninety-nine percent match," Jon says.

Charlie releases a hard breath. "Yep. They were listening."

"We have to tell my mom and dad." This from Ethan who stops talking and looks at Jon. "Well, Jon's, I guess."

Ugh. The statement is like a white, hot knife to my heart. "They're still yours, Ethan." I shake my head. "They raised you and love you. No matter what, they always will."

When he doesn't answer, I open my mouth. What can I possibly say that might make a damned difference?

I have no idea what I'm doing. Anything I say could be wrong, so I close my mouth again.

Charlie reaches across the console and squeezes my arm. "Here's what I think. This won't stay contained long. Let's grab food and head home. We'll call Carl and Lily on the way and have them meet us there. Then we'll all talk." She angles back to Jon. "And you'll meet your biological parents."

27

Charlie

I hate fast food, so I pick at a salad while Jon and Ethan inhale burgers, fries, dessert pies, and refill their cups twice at the restaurant. Ethan tells Jon about his new name, and they discuss sports, which leads to computer games.

They're acting like normal teenagers. Under the circumstances, I have to give them credit for lightening the situation. They've even gotten Meg to smile and laugh several times.

The last thing I want to do is talk to Lily, so I plan to call Carl and see how he wants to handle the meet and greet.

Meg is cleaning up when Taylor calls. "What can I do for you, agent?" I ask.

"Where are the boys? Child services is stepping in."

Like hell. "Good for them. Meg and I have DNA proof Jon is Carl's son. I plan to call him so they can meet this afternoon."

There is a frustrated sigh on the other end. "That's for the

FBI to handle, Charlie. You have no legal guardianship of Jon, or Ethan, since he's not Carl and Lily's biological son. JJ's office will be sorting out the legalities. You have to turn both over to us. Once there is an *official* DNA analysis and match, I'll be the one to handle the meeting between the Havers and their son."

The boys have fallen silent. Meg has stopped and is staring at me with fierce protection in her eyes.

I'm probably going to pay for this, but my transgression list is so long already, I find it doesn't faze me.

"These boys have been through enough," I tell Taylor. "There's no reason to make the transition harder than it has to be. If either of them want child services to come get them, I'll contact you." They exchange a wild look, both shaking their heads at me. "Until then, they're staying with my sister. I will contact Carl and let him know what's going on and where he can meet his son, if he so chooses, before this goes any farther. Have you gotten anything else out of Susie?"

There is a long, pregnant pause. She's debating whether to argue with me, threaten to throw me in jail, or possibly worse. In the strained silence, I sense her considering the option of shooting me.

I would too, in her shoes.

Finally, she says, "She lawyered up, and claims this was all Amelia's fault. They both wanted babies and Amelia had a pretty good game going, at least with Ethan. Apparently, the mother in Santa Monica paid her a chunk of money to take him and leave. I don't know why she didn't simply give him up for adoption, but at this point, I can't take anything Susie says as truth. She could just be talking in circles."

"Thank you for sharing that." I know it's taking all her patience not to yell at me. "Since Lily is suing me, we're taking the boys to Meg's. They'll be safe and I'll stay out of the picture if Carl wants to bring Lily to meet their real son. I'm sure they'll want to talk to Ethan as well."

Another long pause, as if Taylor is debating telling me something. "Jackie feels horrible she had to drop you. We had to make sure we avoid any impropriety since this is already loaded with potential landmines. The FBI is dotting Is and crossing Ts on this. We can't afford any other screw ups. I hope you understand."

I do. "Jackie is a professional, as I know you are, and I appreciate what both of you have done for me. I know your hands are tied, but just so you know, it still sucks."

I hang up before she can say anything else. "Let's go."

As much as I like Taylor, she's a federal agent and I'm not convinced child services isn't on their way to find these boys. I want to get moving before that happens.

Everybody jumps up and we make sure to finish cleaning our table before leaving. As we're piling into the BMW, I notice a mother with two young kids staring at us, probably having seen us on the news. I ignore her and we take off. I wonder if I'll ever be able to go anywhere again without public scrutiny.

"Maybe now Lily will get off your back and not sue you," Meg says.

"Doubtful. She threw down the gauntlet on national television. She can't give up now."

"We'll talk to her," Jon volunteers from the back. A glance in my rearview shows Ethan nodding in agreement. "She'll be so happy to have me again, she'll forget all about suing you."

I appreciate their somewhat innocent take on the situation. "I'm really sorry this happened to you guys, and I have to give you full credit for being so mature about this."

They smile awkwardly. Ethan shares an earbud with Jon and they start listening to some of his favorite music. I look at Meg and she smiles at me. I return it.

"So what's going on with Jerome?" I ask as we head east like normal sisters.

A startled expression crosses her face before she pointedly turns to look out her window. "What do you mean?"

"I may have been a little preoccupied the past few days, but I'm not blind. You've had this weird air about you ever since he showed up yesterday. Did he ask you out or something?"

She clears her throat. "Or something."

I glance over and see her smiling in a totally different way. "Are you blushing?"

She rolls her eyes and I laugh. "Come on, Meg. Fess up."

"We've been sort of stuck for a while. Just friends, you know?"

I stay silent, understanding that feeling all too well.

"I trust him," she says. "He's kind."

"Not to mention good-looking," I throw in, teasingly.

She punches me in the bicep half-heartedly. "He's definitely my type. But he's such a good friend, I don't want things to get weird between us."

The Schock sisters have a terrible track record with men, and while we both have a few friends, those are in short supply as well. We have plenty of contacts and acquaintances, but true friends––ones we trust beyond a shadow of a doubt—I can count them on one hand.

Meg and I have always been each other's best friend, and that seems to keep others out. The psychologist in me knows that's probably not the healthiest scenario, but I wouldn't have it any other way. I am not, nor will I ever be, closer to anyone than I am to her.

"I'd offer advice," I tell her, "but I'm not exactly an expert, in case you haven't noticed."

We share a laugh and she falls silent, probably thinking about Jerome and where she's going with him.

For the first time in days, I feel a little less filled with doom and gloom. My sister is having boyfriend troubles, the two in the back are talking about music and acting like normal teenagers. I feel like calling my dad later and having a mundane conversation about the weather or politics.

I put my problems on hold, allowing myself a few minutes to relax as I drive us home.

A cruiser sits across the street from our duplex, still keeping the press at bay, and I'm grateful. Meg takes the boys to her side of our shared house, and I sit in my car and call Carl.

"I have your son," I tell him, my mind flashing back to eight years ago when I said the same words to him. "I have a DNA match. I know for sure he's yours, Carl."

Dead silence echoes through the connection, and then I hear very soft crying. I give the man time to process the truth.

It doesn't take long for him to pull himself together. "Who is he? *Where* is he?"

"His name is Jon and he's at my sister's." I rattle off the address. "You and Lily are welcome to come when you're ready, although you won't be granted custody until an official match is completed."

"Lily's at the studio. She goes on air in a few minutes. I suppose I should wait for her so we can meet him together."

"That decision is up to you. I doubt it'll be long before the truth is leaked to the press, so you may want to get over here soon. I know both boys have a lot to talk about with you."

A heavy sigh. "Thank you."

"They'll be waiting when you're ready."

We disconnect and I let Meg know Carl and Lily should be by later. "I'll stay at my place if you can handle it. No point provoking Lily and I might try to kill her if she smarts off at me."

"I can do it," she says, "but I'll call you if I need backup."

Jon comes to the door and hugs me. "Thank you," he says, echoing his father's earlier statement. I try not to tear up.

Ethan follows and gives me a fist bump. "Same goes for me. I'm just hoping we can figure out who my real parents are."

I clasp him on the shoulder and squeeze. "I won't quit until I find them. That's a promise."

I leave them to wait for Carl and Lily and go to my place to follow up on George's results.

28

Meg

I'm sitting at my kitchen table checking emails on my tablet when my doorbell rings.

This might be it.

My stomach flips and I set my hand there like that would help. *Dream on.*

The boys are on the living room sofa watching a movie on the Sci-Fi channel and to make sure one of them doesn't get antsy and try to beat me to the door, I hustle in.

Jon is on his feet. I point at him. "Don't even think about it."

For all we know, it could be a rogue reporter.

I check the security app on my phone and see Carl on my tiny porch.

It's happening. Right now.

I take a deep breath and shoot my sister a text. She'd already made it clear she's staying away while I moderate the reunion. An hour ago I was fine with it. Now? My pulse is kicking so hard I might fall over.

As I open the door a burst of voices sounds from across the street. The cops are doing a fine job keeping the dozen reporters off our property, but we don't own the sidewalk and can't kick them out.

I quickly wave Carl in, limiting the amount of photos and video.

By the time I get the door closed, the television has been muted and a heavy silence descends. Ethan and Jon are on their feet, frozen and staring at Carl. Ethan's gaze flicks to me and for the first time, I sense a bit of frenzied panic.

This poor kid has been through so much. I can't believe it's taken him this long to lose his cool.

I move past Carl, heading straight for the boys. "Carl, come in." I set one hand on Jon's arm. "Jon, this is..." Lord, what am I supposed to say? *This is your father? Carl? Your sperm donor?*

Kill me. Please.

I look at Carl, the man who's been in front of a camera his whole career. If he's nervous, I don't see it. Something I'm insanely grateful for on behalf of my young friends beside me.

Carl nods and steps forward, hand extended. "I'm...Carl. From what I hear, I'm your biological father."

Hardly a Hallmark moment, but, well, it is what it is.

The handshake is quick and all business and, as someone who's known—and loved—her biological father, I wonder what this must feel like to not just Jon and Carl, but to Ethan. He's watching the man he's known as Dad, meet his true son.

Jon slides his hand from Carl's but keeps his gaze steady on the man he so strongly resembles.

But Carl's attention has moved to Ethan. "Hello, son. I've missed you."

God, whatever mistakes this man has made, at this moment

I can't remember a single one. He's put his own emotions aside and made it all about these boys.

I hold my hands out. "Let's all have a seat. How about something to drink?" *Or maybe a pot brownie?* "I have lemonade."

Carl nods. "That sounds good."

I head into the kitchen and put a tray together with cookies. My inventory is dismally limited, but I do enjoy my sweets and always have butter cookies on hand.

By the time I return, the boys are giving Carl a full update on the day's events, all of them talking like old friends.

I set the tray down. "Help yourselves."

They continue to peer at me and the awkward silence returns. Suddenly, I'm the outsider in this little reunion.

I get it. They need time to talk without an audience. Without someone who is a partner in a PI agency.

"Boys," I say, "how about I give you some privacy. Would that be okay?"

Ethan and Jon exchange a look and communicate in some sort of teenage language I'm way too old to understand.

"Yeah," Ethan says. "That'd be good."

I turn to Carl. "I'll be right next door."

Rather than go out the front and give the reporters a photo op, I head out back.

Fresh air wraps around me and I note that my morning meditation has long since worn off.

Three minutes. That's all I need to ground myself. To get focused and recharge.

I sit on the rattan high-backed chair that has become my sanctuary on nice days and prop my feet on the ottoman.

A bird tweets and I rest my head back, breathing deeply as I close my eyes. A light wind caresses my cheeks and...yes...my body begins to loosen.

"Meg?"

Charlie's voice.

So much for my three minutes. I open my eyes, see my sister standing over me, her blond hair backlit by streaming sun.

I check the time on my phone. I've been sitting here at least ten minutes. I must've fallen asleep. Dammit.

"Hi," I croak. "Sorry. I was coming to update you, but needed a second."

"It's all right. I saw you sitting out here and wasn't sure what happened. Is everything okay?"

Shaking off the fog in my brain, I nod. "Carl got here about fifteen minutes ago. They're inside. Talking."

"It's a good sign if you're sitting out here."

"It seemed to be going okay. I sensed the boys wanted privacy."

"Where's Lily?"

"Still at work, I assume. He didn't say." I stand and give my neck a stretch. "I'm going to check on them. Want to come inside?"

Charlie peers at my door, her longing to enter evident. I sense her protective instincts being brutally smothered as she shakes her head. "I should steer clear. But call if you need me."

My poor sister. She's been submerged in this case for days, pushing people's buttons and digging up info from every conceivable angle and is now forced to step back. Whatever happens with Lily and this damned lawsuit, Charlie will get the credit due for finding the real Ethan.

I'll make sure of it.

29

Charlie

*S*everal hours later, I still have no final results to prove George is Ethan's father.

The lab in California is dragging its feet because there's no pressure on them yet. Taylor would do it, except she's still wrapped up with Susie and that fiasco.

Carl is still at Meg's. Lily has yet to show up.

I had a brief call with my father and brought him up to date. Matt stopped by and dropped off JJ. He's currently making pasta.

The smell of garlic and onion makes my stomach growl, since I ate little of my salad earlier. Trouble is, my mind keeps circling back to all my issues and making my stomach flip-flop. One second I'm hungry, the other I want to throw up. It's probably all the stress and worry finally catching up with me.

JJ pours me a glass of wine, and I stare at it, wanting to drink but knowing my stomach won't let me.

I hate waiting. I pick up the phone and call the first attorney Jackie gave me. I get the man's receptionist, who tells me he's in a meeting and will call me back.

I debate trying the second to see if I can get a faster response. This one's a woman and I'm hoping she's just like Jackie, so I do. I'm told she, too, is busy but will return my call by the end of the day.

The biggest worry I have is that George's DNA is not a match for Ethan. What then?

If nothing else, I have to figure out who his parents are. I'm running out of time before some judge forces Meg to give him up to child services, and I'll be damned if I let that happen.

"Stop stewing." JJ appears at the dining room table to refill my glass, sees it's still full. "These things take time."

"I'm not a patient person."

He pours a glass of the wine and takes a sip. "You don't have to tell me that."

I stare at the dark red liquid. I've never been much of a drinker, but suddenly I want to down the whole damned bottle, regardless of my fluky stomach. "I still haven't found Ethan's real parents, I'm being sued, you're on suspension, and I don't have a lawyer. I've got a long way to go before I can see the light of day."

"You're tired and hungry. You'll feel better after I feed you."

"Have you heard from your wife?" The words fly out before I can stop them, as if I've already lost my inhibitions from simply looking at the wine.

He turns and walks to the kitchen. I hear the *whack whack whack* of the knife on the cutting board. "Don't worry about her. I'll handle it."

Which means they're going back to the drawing board. Of course, she's going to take him to the cleaners now that she has proof—at least circumstantial evidence—that JJ has been having an affair while they were married.

I take a long drink of the alcohol finally. My stomach doesn't revolt. I take another swig.

Lost in my own thoughts, damning myself once again, I don't notice when JJ returns. I jump when he sets a platter of chopped vegetables and sliced bread in front of me. "Eat," he commands.

I'd rather just drink, now that I'm on a roll. My brain's getting a little fuzzy, thanks to my empty stomach, and it's slowing my thoughts. A little more and I can curl up in bed and forget about everything.

"I've spent all these years working to get to this point—running my own business, helping people, doing it all with my sister. One mistake, and I've ruined everything, not just for me but for her and you. Hell, even Matt. If we have to close our doors, he and Haley will lose their jobs. If Lily takes me to court, my savings will be completely wiped out, and who's going to hire me for a job? Can you imagine if I have to move home with Mom and Dad? Ugh."

I hang my head, embarrassed to be admitting all of this to anyone, especially JJ. I don't usually get this morose about anything—I'm a warrior, a survivor. Nothing has ever brought me this low.

"Hey, look at me."

He sits across from me and sets his elbows on the table. He's got that look—the one I've seen him use to get his way with clients, judges, other lawyers. "You don't need me to give you a pity party. You're better than that. You need me to tell you to do what you do and screw your demons. You can—and will—handle whatever comes, and you'll do it like a pro. Always have and always will. If you need me, I'm here, but I know you. You've got this, Charlie."

His belief in me is unwavering. I'm not sure what I've done to deserve it, but I let the words sink in as I take a piece of bread and nibble. I want to kiss him, but if I stand too quickly, I might topple over.

The bread is delicious, and I'm definitely hungry now. "My mind keeps circling back to something Susie said in the parking lot. 'She only took the babies whose mothers didn't want them.' That's what she said about Amelia."

JJ gets up and goes to the kitchen, returning moments later with two plates piled full of spaghetti. "Why is that bothering you?"

"Is that what Amelia told herself and her sister so she didn't feel guilty about taking other people's children? That they didn't want them?"

He shrugs, staying silent to let me work through this, and we dig in. The sauce is good, the pasta done to perfection, and I'm suddenly ravenous. "This is delicious."

He raises his glass and I clink mine against it, staring at him over the rim as I sip. He stares back at me, and I feel that delicious electricity between us.

I eat more pasta, tear apart another piece of bread and wolf that down. "I keep thinking about what Susie confessed to Taylor—the mother in Santa Monica paid Amelia. Why? If the mother didn't want her kid, wouldn't she give it up for adoption? There are so many couples out there who want children, why would anyone pay someone like Amelia to take their baby away?"

In my years working for the FBI and profiling criminals, I've seen and heard a lot of strange things. Mental health is often times the source behind unusual, illogical behavior.

Money and greed, power, unhealthy relationships—they round out the other reasons.

Wine in hand, I think about money and power struggles. About a pregnant woman paying another to take—or kidnap? —her baby.

Meg texts. *Lily's not coming. She texted Carl and said she didn't want to have her heart broken all over again if Jon isn't hers. Ordering pizza now. Want to come over?*

Oh Lily. You drama queen. I told Carl we had the DNA test, proving Jon was his. It may not be admissible in court, but it's still accurate. "Well, at least Carl and Jon have met," I tell JJ.

"No Lily?"

I shake my head.

"Do they want to join us? There's plenty to go around."

While that's the considerate thing to do, I'd rather sit and brainstorm with the handsome, although tired, looking guy across from me. I think both of us could use some downtime.

I reply. *Having dinner now. JJ made spaghetti. Want the leftovers?*

A minute later, she responds. *The boys want pizza, but I'd love some, if you have extra.*

I'll have him bring you a plate in a little bit.

She sends me a thumbs-up emoticon.

Money, money, money. Something niggles at my brain. I eat more pasta and then, as lightning strikes, I jump up and run to my office.

"What is it?" JJ calls after me.

I return with one of the files I still have from the original case. "When we went through Amelia's house after we found Ethan, she had two suitcases packed––one for her, the other for him. There was a false bottom in hers and ten thousand dollars in large bills under it."

He whistles softly and motions at me to go on. "So?"

"She had those bags in case she had to leave in a hurry. I figured for a get out of town quick emergency. She had a bank account, but only used it to pay bills. No savings. No credit cards. She lived paycheck to paycheck on minimum wage, yet the house was in a nice, middle-class neighborhood."

JJ finishes a fork full of pasta and shrugs. "She was living under a false name after she kidnapped a baby. Makes sense she'd be ready to run if anyone found out."

I flip through my notes, reading quickly. "She had no mortgage because she rented, but she also had no car payment. She must've used cash for the car, and her rent was over a thousand dollars a month, which she also paid in cash when she had a child to raise and no one to help her financially? It doesn't make sense."

He and I once more stare at each other across the table. "You think she used the money the California mother paid her to buy the car and rent the house?"

"And for new identities and travel expenses for herself, the baby, and her sister. Yet, she still had ten thousand dollars in cash. That adds up to a hell of a lot."

"Maybe that wasn't the only child she was paid to take? Or she had a longer history of buying and selling children?"

That's what I'm afraid of. The kid we know as Ethan might not have been the first child Amelia and Susie brokered. He might not be the last they stole. "I need to talk to Susie."

JJ makes a huffing noise. "You know that's not going to happen. Call Taylor. Let her go down that rabbit hole."

I try to remember Amelia, the woman I saw and talked to for only moments before she killed herself. She had a quiet, simple beauty like her sister. She seemed completely normal, in fact, no hint of mental issues, but they're rarely obvious when you first meet someone.

I remember her self-righteous indignation that we'd come to take Ethan away. That anyone could love him more than she did.

I also recall the look on her face when she realized the gig was up. Her fury that her neighbor had fingered her as Ethan's kidnapper. The way she seemed to care more about herself than him, despite her claims that she loved him.

Lily's face flashes across my mind. That same righteous indignation and anger covering up her fear.

My phone rings and it's Matt. "We've got a match on Ethan."

"George?"

"The very one. Ethan is his son, but there are no missing children reports that match the date, time, and place. If he was kidnapped, his mother didn't report it. Do you think Amelia is actually the mother?"

"No. My theory is the mother paid Amelia to take him, based on things Susie told us."

A pause. "You know that sounds ass backwards, right? Why would anyone do that?"

"No idea, but I need to talk to Taylor. Is she with you?"

"She's still at the Bureau. I'm at the office. Do you want me to call her?"

My dinner's getting cold, but I know I'm onto something, no matter how ridiculous it sounds. "Nah, you go home. I'll talk to her as soon as I have solid information."

I sink back in my chair with some relief. "We found Ethan 's father."

JJ smiles. "That's great. See? I knew you'd figure it out."

I'm not done yet. "Do you remember how Lily's popularity shot into the stratosphere when she was pregnant?"

JJ has finished his food and he kicks back, wiping his fingers on his napkin. "Sure. That's when she and Carl became America's sweethearts."

"Within a few weeks after she had the baby, the public moved on, like they always do. She was on maternity leave and Carl was still in the spotlight."

"Where are you going with this?"

I'm already dialing Taylor. When she answers, I say, "You need to check Carl and Lily's finances from fifteen years ago when their baby was born."

Taylor's voice is strained, tired. "Why?"

"Because if you look hard enough, I think you'll find a money trail that links Lily to Amelia. I found the fake Ethan's biological father in California where Amelia and Susie lived before they came to D.C. The mother paid Amelia to take the child and disappear, and he wasn't the only one Amelia did this with."

"What are you saying, Charlie?"

"Lily paid Amelia to kidnap her son."

30

Charlie

"You've been under a lot of stress," Taylor says to me, once more forced to find patience. "You're not making sense."

Lily loves the spotlight, would do almost anything to stay in it. She lives on drama that she plays out in front of the world.

"Will you promise me you'll look into it? Please, Taylor. I know there's a connection."

Her response comes a little too fast, and drips with sarcasm. "It's not like I have anything else to do. You're lucky Matt loves you in a platonic, sisterly type of way."

She hangs up and I toss the phone on top of my file. "I need to fax her my notes."

JJ points at my plate. "Finish your dinner. Nothing else is going to get done tonight."

He's right, but I itch to force something to happen anyway.

I know he won't let me go anywhere until I eat, so I begin scarfing it down. It's good, and I'm so glad he made it for me.

We bat around ideas to explain my theory. It's challenging. To us, it makes no sense for someone to give their child away with a lump sum of money. "Unless the mother feels guilty and wants to make sure the baby is well taken care of," I say, swallowing a mouthful.

JJ starts to clean up, sliding a couple of carrot and celery pieces onto my plate. He doesn't resemble my mother, but I'd swear he's channeling her. "I can see that as a possibility."

"Especially if the mother doesn't want anyone to find out. The money helps to hush up the kidnapper—although technically it's not kidnapping if you give the baby away."

"Still a crime, under the circumstances." In the kitchen, he loads the dishwasher, and puts the leftover noodles and sauce into a bowl to take to Meg. "I can't see why Lily would want someone to take her child. Publicity stunt? Did she want them to return him later? Not too smart since the FBI would've been all over tracking down the person, right?"

"Right." I think back to the day I returned a seven-year-old boy to her and Carl. The look on her face I assumed was happy shock might've just been shock. "I wonder why Amelia stayed in D.C. afterwards. Did Lily know?"

"Maybe that was the deal," JJ says, wrapping garlic bread slices in foil to take with the pasta. "Maybe she wanted Ethan around so she could keep checking on him, and she never realized the boy she thought was Ethan wasn't hers."

This is sounding even more bizarre. "I've seen narcissists who would do almost anything to keep everyone's attention on them, feeling they deserved love more than anyone else in their life. At this point, there's not much that could astonish me about this case."

"I'll run this to Meg. Why don't you open a fresh bottle for us?"

In his eyes, I see the promise of tomorrow. A thousand of them. "I think I'll change into something more comfortable while you're gone. Don't be long."

He's slightly surprised by the invitation, but he's smart. He knows better than to look a gift horse in the mouth. He leans over and kisses me. "Be right back."

With everyone's help, I've solved the most crucial aspects of the case—discovering both boys' real identities. I hope I'm wrong about Lily, that I'm not about to rip her away from Jon just when he's found her.

I finish my wine before I go to the bathroom to change and hear a knock at the back. Thinking JJ has locked himself out, I hustle over to glance out the bedroom window. I can't see the person's face from this angle, but it's not tall enough to be JJ.

I catch sight of jeans and a sports jacket, and I think it must be one of the boys. Meg probably wants some parmesan for her spaghetti.

Thank goodness I'm still in my street clothes, I think, as I open the door, smiling. It quickly fades. "What do you want?"

Twilight has fallen, a coolness in the air. Lily's tucked her hair under a ball cap. Her face is in shadow as she looks at me solemnly from under the brim. "I came to apologize. Carl told me everything. I'm on my way to see Jon."

That's an unexpected turnabout. "No camera crew to record it?" I can't help the snark. She probably came to the back door in order to avoid the cameras. "Apology accepted. Now go away. I have nothing to say to you."

"I'm dropping the lawsuit. I wanted to tell you in person."

A tinge of relief washes through me. "Glad to hear it. Go see your son. Goodnight."

I start to close the door, but she puts out a hand and stops it. "I know you're angry, and you have every right to be, but I'm serious. I'm sorry. You don't understand what it's like when somebody screws up your life, especially when it comes to your child—the person you gave birth to. He was my everything."

She's serious, dark eyes pleading for my forgiveness.

"I hope everything works out for all of you. They're both good kids, and I hope you'll still be there for the one you've raised the past eight years. He may need you more than ever the next few weeks, as he gets to know his real father and transitions to a new family."

I try once more to close the door, but she won't let go, continuing to strong-arm it. "My life wasn't supposed to go like this, you know?"

I wish I could interrogate her about Amelia, but I have no proof and this is not the time nor the place to get into it with her. That's Taylor's job.

Yet, if Lily is the type of woman I believe her to be, and she's about to be exposed for having a hand in her son's kidnapping, there's no telling what she might do. Those with clinical narcissistic personality disorder have several common traits including lack of remorse, the ability to be cleverly deceptive, and sometimes display a Jekyll and Hyde personality.

Above everything else, they tend to believe they're entitled. Whatever they want should be theirs, regardless if it hurts anyone else.

"How should it have gone, Lily?"

A normal person would mention the twists and turns of the kidnapping. What Lily says chills me to the bone. "No one was supposed to know, but you figured it out, didn't you?"

Warning bells peal in my head. "You need to leave."

I bring my elbow down on her arm, breaking her hold. She throws her body against the door, taking me off guard. I stumble and kick out, catching her in the shin.

She cries out and I start to slam the door into her body, but the next thing I know, I'm staring at the end of a gun barrel.

The deadly click of the cocking mechanism sounds too

loud in my ears. "You've ruined everything, you goddamn bitch."

I step back, raising both hands in a supplicating gesture. My gun is in the bedroom, too far away, but if I get her inside, I can distract her. There are plenty of things I can use as a weapon.

"I have no idea what you're talking about, Lily. Why don't we go next door and meet Jon? He's excited to finally know his real mother."

She steps inside, aiming at my chest. "Agent Sinclair asked me to come and see her. She said the two of you were going over the original files and found discrepancies. She started asking about Amelia Norris and how much I paid her to babysit."

"I have no idea what that's about," I lie. I hear the quiet creak of the front door opening and know JJ is back, but there's no way to warn him without alerting Lily. "Would you like me to call Taylor and have her explain it to us?"

Lily chuckles under her breath, not seeming to have heard the noise I'm so used to. "I'm sure Susie is filling in the blanks for everyone. My whole life, everything I've worked so hard for, is going down the tubes. There's no reason for me to live. I'll be crucified in the public eye. All my fans—they're going to abandon me."

"Why did you do it?"

"Publicity, what else? The only problem is, I was supposed to get Ethan back. Susie ran off with him and left that other boy behind. Amelia wanted me to take him, but how could I? He wasn't my son. And then, look at you, Miss Federal Agent. You brought him to me anyway and I had to pretend he *was* mine."

"Charlie?" JJ calls. "Who are you talking to?"

"Go back to Meg's," I yell, but of course, he doesn't.

"What the...?" He's standing a few feet behind me in the living room doorway. His face goes from surprise to calm reassurance. "Hi, Lily. Put the gun down. You don't want to do this."

He thinks she's going to shoot me. Maybe she is, but she also plans to shoot herself. "He's right. It doesn't have to end like this. Whatever you've done, there are still two young men next door that want you in their lives. They need you."

She gives me a sad smirk. "I only planned to take you with me, but I guess I'll have to kill him too."

Before I can react, she turns on JJ.

Bam.

By the time the bullet hits him, I've jumped her. Taking her to the ground, I wrestle with her gun hand to keep it from pointing at me. She grunts, it goes off again, and a bullet punches into the ceiling.

Plaster rains down on us as we roll over and over. I land an elbow to her ribs, a knee into her groin. She slaps at me, pulls my hair. Screams obscenities.

Lily fights like a girl.

Still, she has raw fury driving her. I've ruined her plans and she's not one to go down without hurting me back.

JJ. It's all I think, his name a chant in my head.

Raw fury isn't only Lily's territory. It courses through my body like wildfire. I overpower her and slam her hand on the floor multiple times, knocking the gun loose. Once more, she fights back, teeth gritted, but I'm in a blind rage.

I punch her in the face—once, twice, three times. She stops moving, blood pouring from her nose, and my knuckles.

She's unconscious, and my chest heaves. I throw myself off her and run to JJ. He's lying on his back, bright red blood spreading across his shirt.

Falling to my knees, I stifle a sob. His eyes flutter open and he tries to look at me.

"You're okay," I tell him. I press my hand over the wound, as if I can stop him from bleeding out by sheer will. "I'm going to save you."

He tries to lift his hand, fingers hovering in the air as he reaches for me. I need to call 911, but all I can do is grasp his fingers and pull them to my chest.

"Charlie," he huffs.

"I need to grab my phone and call an ambulance, but you're going to be fine."

I hear the front door open and close. "Charlie?" Meg calls.

"Call 911!" I scream. "JJ's shot. Phone's on the table."

She runs in, swearing as she takes in me, JJ, and a still unconscious Lily. She doesn't ask questions—bless her—and disappears into the dining room.

JJ's lips move, but I can't hear what he's saying. I lean down, Meg's voice filtering in as she gives the operator the address and tells her a man's been shot.

"Don't talk," I tell JJ. "They're on the way."

The damn man never listens to me, even when he's bleeding from a gunshot wound. "I...love you...Charlize."

It's the last thing he says before falling unconscious.

31

Meg

JJ is stable and in recovery after a complicated surgery that removed a bullet from his torso. During my work as a forensic sculptor, I've heard about wounds to the midsection. Many times, it proves fatal.

Thank God is all I can think as darkness and the bright overhead street lights of the expressway surround me.

It's late, I'm exhausted and have no business—zero—heading to Jerome's.

Not the way I'm feeling—needy and desperate for comfort. But seeing my sister on her knees beside a wounded JJ triggered something in me. Something intense.

Primal.

Charlie and JJ haven't had one of those white-picket romances. If you ask me, it's a fucked-up one. What with his wife and all.

Twisted as it is, there's a connection between them. An

unbreakable bond that I've only experienced with one man. As I watched blood pour from JJ, all I could think about was Jerome and life without him.

So, here I am, darkness be damned, with my foot heavy on the gas pedal.

I park in front of his apartment where the lights are off. That could mean several things: he's asleep; he has a woman in there; he's not home.

The dashboard clock reads eleven-forty-seven. I'm going with option one—and praying like hell I don't run face first into some ho when I'm about to pour my heart out to this man.

I push the door open only half guilt-ridden about possibly waking him up. What I have to say can't wait. Hopefully, he won't be mad at me for delaying my answer.

Before I even reach the door, a light comes on, jerking me out of my thoughts.

Jerome swings it open and the bare bulb that constitutes an overhead hallway light shines down on his rumpled hair. He's wearing basketball shorts and nothing else and oh...his lean, ropey muscles are exceptionally yummy to my fatigued eyes.

His gaze locks on mine as he steps back, granting me access. "Are you okay?"

He flips a switch, illuminating the small living room, but before he can do much else, I spin around, go on tiptoes and slap my hand over the back of his neck.

His eyes widen as I move in and kiss him with everything I've got. After the last few days, he feels warm and comfortable and...*home.*

I have no desire to end this supremely magnificent moment and since he's not exactly running away, our contact lingers. He pulls me closer, crushing me against him. If I let it, I know what'll happen. We'll wind up in his bedroom, which wouldn't be a bad thing, but it's not what I'm here for so I jump back and, chest thumping, hold my hands up.

"No."

"No?"

"Well, yes, but no."

He sighs. "Meg, help me out here. It's late, you left me hanging and I'm tired. On a normal day, you confuse me. Right now? We're in Twilight Zone territory."

Fully acknowledging I've been crappy to him, I nod. "I'm sorry. I should have said...something. You deserve that and more. But...I'm not here for sex."

His eyebrows hitch up a fraction. "O-kay."

"But I don't want to be stuck anymore either."

Before he can respond, I charge ahead, letting the words, everything I'm feeling tumble out. "Something happened tonight and I never—ever—want to take you for granted again."

Concern darkens his eyes and he reaches for me, dragging me to him and squeezing. "What is it? Are you hurt?"

My cheek is pressed against his bare chest and all that warm, hard skin.

Home.

"No. It's JJ. He got shot."

"Holy shit."

"He'll be okay. He just got out of surgery, but Charlie, oh my God, she was so scared."

The pounding in my chest ramps up—*boom, boom, boom.* My heart is slamming so hard it steals my breath and I step away again, shaking my head. I know how this goes. If I don't get control of myself, I'll be on the floor in a full-blown panic attack.

Jerome clasps my hands. "Sit. Right now. Head between your knees. I'm here, Meg. Just...breathe."

He's here.

Funny how the very thing that brought me to him and his pot brownies was the thing happening at this moment.

I drop to his couch and do as he said. From the sounds of it, he's in the tiny galley kitchen getting water.

Seconds later, my body lists sideways after he sits next to me. He caresses my back, up and down, up and down. Gentle, even strokes that settle my rioting thoughts and it's so perfect. Beyond perfect.

One, two, three. I count each breath, focusing on steady exhalations. By the time I reach ten, my heart rate has slowed enough where I can sit straight.

Still, Jerome touches me. "You're okay," he says. "I'm here. Just relax."

Leaning into him, I take every bit of comfort he's willing to give. Selfish, I know, but I'll make it up to him.

I squeeze in closer, tucking myself into him.

Home.

"I have so much to tell you."

"There's time."

No. There isn't. I'm so sick of being afraid. Finally, I sit tall and face him, stare at him straight in the eyes because I won't come unstuck without looking at him. "I'm sorry for leaving you hanging. You didn't deserve that. I was scared and well, thrown. I knew I wanted to say yes to you. To thank whatever God brought you into my life, but fear took over."

"I'm scared, too. More so of staying where we are."

After witnessing what Charlie and JJ just went through, I somehow understand. "I was so worried about losing your friendship, I didn't even consider what could happen. That maybe you'd step off a curb and get hit by a bus and I'll have spent these last couple years never allowing myself to love you. To *really* love you. The way you should be. That's what I want. You and whatever life we can carve out."

I stop talking. Charlie always likes to say the first person to speak during a negotiation loses. This isn't one, but I'm definitely trying to win.

His silence sends another wave of panic whipping through me. *He's done. He doesn't want me. He's still pissed.*

I drop my chin to my chest and wait for him to shatter my world. I'd deserve it after running away from him yesterday.

"I'm so sorry," I say.

"Hey, look at me."

Here it comes. Whatever he's about to say, I can't fall apart. This is my doing and I refuse to make him feel guilty about it. I push my shoulders back and lift my head. "It's okay."

He shakes his head and lets out a little laugh. "Of course it is. What do you think? That I'm going to be a dick and throw you out because you were scared? You know me better."

His words reach me and I blink. Did he say? Does he mean?

"Is that a...yes?"

He kisses me. This time he's the one putting everything he has into it and an explosion of energy overcomes every bit of fatigue weighing me down.

By the time he pulls back, I'm half on top of him and he has an erection that leaves me ready to do wicked things.

We both know where this is going.

That doesn't make it right. Not after all we've been through. The relationship we've built is worth more than a quick lay.

"I want a date," he says. "Dinner and a movie and then I'll bang the hell out of you. Is that...okay?"

Jerome. Mind reader.

Silly tears clog my throat and I nod. "I'd love that. A fresh start."

"Good. Now tell me what the hell happened tonight."

He pulls me onto his lap and I snuggle into him, taking a second to nuzzle his neck.

Peace. After the last few weeks, I'm finally at peace.

32

Charlie

I never realized how much falling in love could hurt.

JJ lies in a cold, sterile hospital bed, the white blanket tucked around him glowing softly under the lights from the monitors. His face is too pale, his body too still.

The prognosis is good, the surgery having gone well to remove the bullet and repair the damage. But all I can think about is the blood. Even now, when I look at my clean hands, I still see it.

My eyes are gritty from trying to hold back tears, and in the relative quiet of the room, with only the beeping monitors surrounding me, I feel a trickle of more roll down my cheek. I dash them away, knowing if I let the dam break, I might not come up for air anytime soon, losing myself in the emotions banging around in my chest.

It was past visiting hours when the nurse came in to tell me to leave. I played nice and begged her to let me stay. JJ's family is on the other side of the continent, and I'm all he's got outside of his soon-to-be ex-wife.

When the nurse didn't relent, I informed her she would have to physically carry me out. She took one look at my face and decided against going to war.

Smart woman. I'll send her a box of chocolates tomorrow.

Of course, JJ's friends and coworkers have been calling, assuring me they'll stop by tomorrow when he's awake and ready for company. Knowing JJ, he'll love the spotlight and turn this event into a good story he can tell over and over.

Me? I'm barely hanging on. While they were operating, I gave my statement to the police, and again to Taylor, and that at least gave my mind something to chew on. Now, Meg and Matt are gone, the intensive care ward has settled down for the night —as much as it ever does in a hospital—and it's just me and my demons watching over the man I love.

Leaning forward, I grab the rails and squeeze, trying to release some anxiety. They're so cold, like my fears. I feel like I could climb the walls, and the psychiatrist in me knows that's due to suppressing emotions.

My love for JJ is too big, too overwhelming. I realized it when I saw him go down, when his blood covered my hands.

When I knew I couldn't save him.

That's what it felt like while we waited for the ambulance— that he was dying because of me. I did my best to stop the bleeding and keep him from going into shock, but it felt like too damn little. I was sure we were going to lose him. *I* was going to lose him.

The scene flashes in my mind again and I grip even harder, making my hands cramp. I stand and pace for the hundredth time.

I probably won't crash for days from all this adrenaline and anxiety, but when I do it'll be a doozy. Too bad the hospital doesn't have a gun range. I could plaster Lily's face on a target and work out some of my anger.

After being taken into custody, she was brought to the ER and had her broken nose reset. I can still remember Jon and Ethan's faces as they watched her being put into a cruiser, handcuffs around her wrists, the media frenzy that ensued. The horror those two boys have been through rocks me to the core.

Against Meg's wishes, Taylor removed both from her care and put them in a safe house with a high level of security to keep the press at bay. By morning, Carl will have full custody of his real son, but right now, he's dealing with the fallout of his wife's crimes.

Hopefully come morning, Ethan will meet his real family too. Matt received George's results about the time Lily shot JJ. They're a match to Ethan, and George is on a red eye on his way here. So far, no leads on his mother, but the search will continue. Matt's picking George up at the airport and taking him to the safe house as soon as he arrives.

I return to JJ's side, wondering when his next dose is scheduled for. He's still under sedation as well, and that's good. I have a lot to tell him when he wakes up, but I'd rather he sleep for now and remain pain-free.

When the door behind me creaks open, I assume it's the nurse delivering those pain meds. Shock registers when I see the last person I expected.

The woman looks just as annoyed to see me. Her red lips screw up for a moment before she comes all the way in and says, "How is he?"

Carlena Gage Carrington appears as fresh as if she just started her day. I, on the other hand, probably look like I've been run over by a bulldozer. I feel like I have, anyway.

"The bullet nicked the bottom of a rib but missed his lung and vital organs. Surgery went well. I suspect he'll be up and around in a couple of days."

She stands at the foot of the bed, staring at JJ, and I can see real emotion behind her perfect features. "He's too stubborn to die."

It sounds harsh, and yet I understand where it comes from. She still has feelings for him, but she's trying to cover them up.

There's a part of me that desperately wants to protect JJ from his wife, and the irony almost makes me laugh. "He's a good man and this is my fault."

"You're at fault for a lot of things, Charlie Schock." She sends me a hateful look. "But I want you to know you're not the reason for our marriage going bad."

I can't tell if she's trying to relieve my guilt or let me know I'm not special enough to ruin it.

I don't really care. "I'm sure there was a time when the two of you were happy. I hope you can remember that, what he was like then. He's a kind and generous person, and I assume you must've been too. Maybe you can find a little of that again and give him what he wants."

The lips screw up once more. "I suppose you mean you?"

"I do." *If he still wants me.*

She taps a foot on the linoleum, glaring at me to see if I'll back down.

I don't.

I doubt JJ's told her anything about me but she should know how tenacious I am just from everything that's been in the news the past week.

She sighs and reaches into her designer handbag, withdrawing a manila envelope. She tosses it on his legs. "Have him call me when he's up for it."

She turns and leaves, and I watch until the door closes behind her before I allow myself to consider what's inside that envelope.

Could it be? No. Talk about tenacious. Carlena would never miss an opportunity to put JJ through the ringer.

Gingerly, I reach out and open the flap. My pulse skitters. I hold my breath as I remove a set of papers.

The words across the top blur and I move closer to the monitors and their sickly yellow illumination to get a better look.

All the adrenaline in my body whooshes out as I realize the gift Carlena has just given me.

I flip to the last couple pages, seeing her signature scrawled on the crucial lines.

JJ shifts and I look up to see him blinking his eyes open.

"Hey." I lean over and kiss his cheek. "How are you feeling?"

He manages to raise a hand and rub it across his face. His voice is rough. "Like you beat the shit out of me."

All the anxiety and worry is gone. *Poof.* I throw my head back and laugh, not so much because it's funny, but just for the release.

"What...happened?" he asks.

Tucking the papers back into the envelope, I put them on the bedside table and resume my seat next to him. He reaches for my hand and I give it to him, leaning forward on my elbows and smiling.

For the next several minutes, I bring him up to speed. By the time I'm done, I feel like the old me—in control, happy, and ready to take on the world. That's what JJ Carrington does to me.

The best thing is, he's all mine now. Thanks to the papers nearby, he's a free man.

"I'm holding you to that date this weekend," I tell him.

He glances down to look at the bandages across his lower chest and abdomen. "I think we might have to eat in."

"No way." I reach over and grab the envelope and hold it up so he can see. "I want everyone to know about our relationship. We're coming out of the closet."

His eyes grow round. "Is that what I think it is?"

I nod, grinning. "Your *ex*"—I emphasize the word —"brought them by a little while ago."

"I can't believe it. How'd you get her to sign?"

If JJ wants to believe I had a hand in pulling off a miracle, I decide not to depose him of that idea. "Hey, nobody messes with Charlie Schock, if they know what's good for them."

He pulls me toward him and gives me a kiss that tastes like the future.

ABOUT THE AUTHORS

USA TODAY bestselling Author Misty Evans has published over fifty novels and writes romantic suspense, urban fantasy, and paranormal romance. Under her pen name, Nyx Halliwell, she also writes small-town cozy mysteries.

When not reading or writing, she enjoys music, movies, and hanging out with her husband, twin sons, and three spoiled rescue dogs. Get your free story and sign up for her newsletter at www.readmistyevans.com. Like her author page on Facebook or follow her on Twitter.

Adrienne Giordano is a *USA Today* bestselling author of over twenty-five romantic suspense and mystery novels. She is a Jersey girl at heart, but now lives in the Midwest with her ultimate supporter of a husband, sports-obsessed son and Elliot, a snuggle-happy rescue. Having grown up near the ocean, Adrienne enjoys paddleboarding, a nice float in a kayak and lounging on the beach with a good book. For more information on Adrienne's books, please visit http://www. AdrienneGiordano.com.

Adrienne can also be found on Facebook at http://www. facebook.com/AdrienneGiordanoAuthor, Twitter at http:// twitter.com/AdriennGiordano and Goodreads at http://www. goodreads.com/AdrienneGiordano. For information on Adrienne's Facebook reader group go to https://www.facebook.com/ groups/AdrienneGiordanoReaderGroup

Dear reader,

Thank you for reading this book. We hope you enjoyed it! If you did, please help others find it by leaving a review at Goodreads or your favorite retailer. Even a few sentences about what you loved about the book will be extremely appreciated!!

Thank you!

Misty & Adrienne

BOOKS BY ADRIENNE GIORDANO

JUSTICE TEAM SERIES w/MISTY EVANS
Stealing Justice
Cheating Justice
Holiday Justice
Exposing Justice
Undercover Justice
Protecting Justice
Missing Justice
Defending Justice

SCHOCK SISTERS MYSTERY SERIES w/Misty Evans
1st Shock
2nd Strike
3rd Tango

THE LUCIE RIZZO MYSTERY SERIES
Dog Collar Crime
Knocked Off
Limbo (novella)
Boosted

Books by Adrienne Giordano

Whacked
Cooked
Incognito

PRIVATE PROTECTOR SERIES
Risking Trust
Man Law
A Just Deception
Negotiating Point
Relentless Pursuit
Opposing Forces

HARLEQUIN INTRIGUES
The Prosecutor
The Defender
The Marshal
The Detective
The Rebel

JUSTIFIABLE CAUSE SERIES
The Chase
The Evasion
The Capture

CASINO FORTUNA SERIES
Deadly Odds

**STEELE RIDGE SERIES w/KELSEY BROWNING
& TRACEY DEVLYN**
Steele Ridge: The Beginning
Going Hard (Kelsey Browning)
Living Fast (Adrienne Giordano)
Loving Deep (Tracey Devlyn)
Breaking Free (Adrienne Giordano)

Roaming Wild (Tracey Devlyn)
Stripping Bare (Kelsey Browning)

STEELE RIDGE SERIES: The Kingstons w/KELSEY BROWNING
& TRACEY DEVLYN
Craving HEAT (Adrienne Giordano)
Tasting FIRE (Kelsey Browning)
Searing NEED (Tracey Devlyn)
Striking EDGE (Kelsey Browning)
Burning ACHE (Adrienne Giordano)

BOOKS BY MISTY EVANS

The Justice Team Series (with Adrienne Giordano)

Stealing Justice

Cheating Justice

Holiday Justice

Exposing Justice

Undercover Justice

Protecting Justice

Missing Justice

Defending Justice

SCHOCK SISTERS MYSTERY SERIES w/Adrienne Giordano

1st Shock

2nd Strike

3rd Tango

SEALS of Shadow Force Series: Spy Division

Man Hunt

Man Killer

Man Down

SEALs of Shadow Force Series

Fatal Truth

Fatal Honor

Fatal Courage

Fatal Love

Fatal Vision

Fatal Thrill

Risk

The SCVC Taskforce Series

Deadly Pursuit

Deadly Deception

Deadly Force

Deadly Intent

Deadly Affair, A SCVC Taskforce novella

Deadly Attraction

Deadly Secrets

Deadly Holiday, A SCVC Taskforce novella

Deadly Target

Deadly Rescue

The Super Agent Series

Operation Sheba

Operation Paris

Operation Proof of Life

The Secret Ingredient Culinary Mystery Series

The Secret Ingredient, A Culinary Romantic Mystery with Bonus Recipes

The Secret Life of Cranberry Sauce, A Secret Ingredient Holiday Novella

CPSIA information can be obtained
at www.ICGtesting.com
Printed in the USA
BVHW042315301019
562569BV00006B/434/P